Table of Contents

Chapter One
Another Friday Morning

With the morning's birth, the sun shines between the flower-patterned blinds onto Violet's face. Like every morning, she didn't appreciate the light's assault on her retinas so early in the day, but she still hadn't bothered to move the bed or to put up her new curtains that she had bought last September. It was now the middle of May, and the snow had nearly all disappeared from the yard. She turns over under the blankets. Violet missed the snow already, she enjoyed being able to mold it into different shapes and structures, and the cool comfort it brought to her. She thought that it made the landscape look pristine. Violet finds herself particularly reluctant to get up for school this morning. She's about to commit to being late when she comes to the realization that it's Friday, and that today was a day off for the school. Violet whips herself out of bed, taking quick yet cautious steps through the mess of clothing and homework on her floor looking for her phone, finding it in Thursday's jeans with a measly eight percent battery left.

Laying back on her bed, phone in hand, she plugs the charger in. She turns over onto her stomach and the fan picks up the back of her shirt with its currents, sending cold air down her back and giving her goose bumps. She opens her phone and checks the camera to see how her hair held up through the night. She finds the reflection looking back at her with pale blue eyes set in the face of a sixteen year old girl with tangled blond hair outlining her visage. The reflection winks at her, and Violet blows a kiss back at it through her light red lips. "It's going to be a good day" she thinks to herself. Remembering that she had made plans with her friend Lilian for this afternoon, Violet sets her phone down on her bed and begins to search through her mess for her clothes of choice. Starting from the bottom of her attire, she grabs a pair of white knee socks with a pink stripe across the toes. She then settles on a purple set of undergarments and a pink skirt that falls to her knees, topping it off with a pink and white spotted tee. She takes her outfit to the washroom with her and sets the various articles on their own hangers for after her shower.

She exits the shower into a misty room after nearly forty minutes and reaches for her towel, drying off quickly and wiping clear the fogged up mirror of her medicine cabinet. After partially re-dressing, so as not to get her shirt wet, the odd droplet of water still running down her body, Violet grabs her brush and runs it through her wet hair for a few minutes. The knots are reluctant to part with their homes, but the persistence of the brush eventually convinces them to straighten out. She dries her hair to get its lighter color back and curls it a bit to make it look especially nice. She dries her shoulders once more and puts her top on. She then continues her daily routine and puts on a bit of makeup; some blush to make her cheeks really pop, a bit of eyeliner to pronounce the blue in her eyes and her red lipstick to pull it all together. Checking the time, Violet is relieved to find that she still has three hours until her and Lilian had planned to meet at the mall.

Violet opens the door to her room, her eyes on her phone, and descends the stairs with finesse, reading up on the mornings of her friends. Lilian had mentioned the day before that she would have a piano recital early this morning, and sure enough, she had posted a short clip from one of her songs. Violet listened to it, and commented congratulating her, mentioning that she was excited for the afternoon to come. Pocketing her phone upon reaching the bottom of the stairs, Violet finds her parents in the kitchen, her mother making an omelet to be split among the family, and her father brewing a cup of coffee for himself, and her little brother at the kitchen table on his computer with his headphones on, music loud enough to be heard from where Violet stood nearly ten feet away. Her parents turn and greet her, her father with a nod and a smile, and her mother with a kindly spoken "Good morning sleepy head! You know it's past noon already, right?" To which Violet responds with "Good morning. Yeah, I couldn't fall asleep until almost three in the morning. How long has he been like that?" she asks, giving a slight flick of the head in the direction of her brother, Peter.

Violet's parents were kind people. Her mother, Diana, was blond like her, but it was a much lighter shade than her own, and her father, Bryan, had light brown hair. Both parents had blue eyes adorned in their sockets. Her mother would be forty three in July, and her father had just turned forty five two weeks ago. Her mother worked at the local hospital as a nurse, and, starting today, she had three days off which she had planned to spend with her kids by taking them to the new zoo that had just opened up nearby. Violet's father ran the town library and had the luxury of being able to take time off as he needed. "He's been there since nine in the morning" Her father replied about Peter.

"You know it's not good to be awake that late, right?" Diana was stuck on her daughters lost sleep.

"Because, you know, I had planned to lay there doing nothing for four hours before I fell asleep, right?" Violet retorted.

"You know I'm just worried about you, so you don't have to use such a harsh tone, girlie."

Violet felt a bit guilty for having spoken the way she did, but to admit that she was in the wrong was too much. She understood her parents only wanted the best for her, but sometimes she just finds them overprotective, and, without intending to, she gets an edge in her voice. "Lilian and I are going to the mall later, in case you're wondering where I'll be. I told you about it yesterday."

"Oh, yeah, I remember you mentioning it. What are you two planning to do? And should we expect you home for dinner?" Diana inquired.

"We're going to meet up around four by the main entrances, to go shopping for a couple hours. We were thinking of going to see a movie afterwards before we leave the mall, so I'll be back maybe around 9:30 tonight."

"Okay, just make sure to call us if you're going to be a bit later than planned, so we don't worry too much."

"Will do."

Once the omelet was ready, Peter moved his computer aside, and their family ate together at the kitchen table. It was quiet as they ate. Bryan finished first and tried to strike up a conversation.

"Are you kids excited to go to the Zoo tomorrow?"

Peter answered first, "Absolutely! I wanna go see the crocodiles and the lions! Do you think we'd be able to see them get fed?"

"Who knows, we might get lucky with our timing and get to." Bryan responds, hiding his concern. "How about you Violet, are you excited to go?"

Violet had begun to pick at her omelet, she had lost her appetite. "Do you think they'll have an aviary?"

"I'd imagine they will, it might be mostly indoors though. It's probably still too cold for most of the birds to be outside."

"That's what I'm looking forward to then."

Bryan was pleased that the kids were at least a little enthusiastic about the trip, it's always a little upsetting when they aren't excited about a trip that he and Diana put so much planning into.

After breakfast, Violet heads back upstairs to finish getting ready. She brushes her teeth and checks over her apparel once more, admiring her lovely pink skirt in the mirror once more. She adored how it twirled when she spun, without it being too revealing. After Violet was completely sure she was ready, she called Lilian to make sure they were still going.

After two rings, Lilian picks up. "Hey, Violet. You know there's only an hour until we meet, right? You're not backing out on me, are you?"

"Definitely, I just wanted to let you know so you wouldn't show up and wait for me." She says sarcastically, rolling her eyes.

"That's a shame, I was really looking forward to this afternoon." Lilian says, going along with it.

"Of course I'm still game, I was wondering the same thing about you, actually."

"Yup, I'm still clear for the afternoon. Where do you wanna go first?"

"Why don't we figure that out once we get there, just in case we change our minds?"

"That's probably a good idea. Well, it's just about time to leave, so I've gotta finish getting ready. I'll see you at the mall. Later V!"

"Okay, see you there Lily!"

Making her way to the front door, she says goodbye to her parents and, throwing a pen at her brother to catch his attention, she waves goodbye to him too. With her coat around her and her purse over her arm, Violet leaves home, shutting the door behind her, and walks off into the chill wind towards the mall.

Chapter Two
Afternoon with Lily

The mall had been built nine years ago, only nine blocks away from where her family lived, and Violet had been very excited even at the age of seven, because a mall to her then meant an amusement park. Now, at sixteen, Violet was still as excited, if not even more so, because now it meant a local shopping complex for her to spend time at with her friends. She mostly enjoyed the clothing stores, because they often had new arrivals that she could try on, even if her budget wouldn't allow for them. She still goes to the amusement park with her friends every few weeks, but their choice in rides had definitely changed. When they were seven, they enjoyed the merry-go-rounds with their parents and the ground level roller coasters. In recent years, they've been slowly making their way up to the bigger roller coasters, because they were all afraid of heights, and the tallest ones were still too much for some of them.

As Violet approached the main doors, she sees Lilian running over to her. "You're cutting it close on time, V! You might wanna start jogging in your off time." Lilian poked.

"You're not exactly an Olympic runner yourself, Miss Hensworth."

"Oooh, pulling out last names are we, Glendale?"

Violet ignored her, "I recall you being late on several occasions yourself."

"But I had good reasons."

"Good and bad is decided by the individual. And besides, I still had three minutes to spare."

The pair were accustomed to this type of banter. It was ritualistic at this point; to nitpick over the little things and tease each other over minute details. They walked alongside one another through the main doors. The theater was the second store on the left from these doors, which was very convenient for the pair, because they wouldn't have to venture as far after their movie.

"So, you said we should decide when we got here. So, where to first?" Lilian asked, more excited now that they were here.

Violet looked around for a minute, thinking where they should start, before asking the question, "How about at Tobi? I heard they got a new shipment in recently."

"They do have some nice looking dresses normally. Sure, let's start there."

***

When they began to make their way to the theater, the two girls each had a bag over one arm, and two over the other. Violet was very happy with the rewards of their trip. Her favorite procuration had its own bag; it was a sleeveless magenta dress that went down to her shins, leaving her shoulders bare and forming a V at the neck, held up by a string that attached to a center piece at the back of her neck that reached out to two spots, one above each shoulder blade. She also bought a cute new purse that had a cartoon cat with a bow behind its left ear on the front that was laying on a navy blue back drop, as well as a few pairs of colorful socks; a green and blue pair that formed a spiral pattern out from the heel, a pair with purple and red poke-a-dots on a white sock, and lastly a pair of black knee socks with pink stripes going down the leg, meeting and forming a circle at the ankle and the knee. The socks shared a bag with a pair of white leggings that had no unique design. Her last bag had a blue bikini with a floral pattern on it, a straw sun hat with a black ribbon around the bend of the hat, and a pair of pink rimmed sunglasses with silver tinted lenses. Her last bag was in preparation for the upcoming summer. While Violet preferred the snow, she was not about to let the summer pass her by without enjoying it. Her parents had a cabin on the lake a little ways out from the city, and she planned to spend more than a couple weeks of her summer there.

Lilian was equally as proud, for she had found an olive colored dress that was a little more reserved than Violet's dress. It went over her shoulders in a billowy frill and outlined her collarbone, its sleeves stop at the elbows, ending in a frill as the shoulders do. Lilian's dress however only falls to the knees, and has an embroidery resembling lilies running across from the waist down. She had two new pairs of skinny jeans and a yellow bikini in the second bag. The third bag contained two scarves; one scarf with spring flowers of pink, yellow, red, orange and white, the second scarf was made of silk and dyed a seafoam green that made you feel calm just looking at it. Along with the scarves, Lily had bought a bright yellow shawl, patterned with rays of sun sprouting from the neck, to cover her up on the beach when she wasn't in the water.

While exchanging compliments about each other's new wardrobe additions, they made their way to the theater. It was six in the afternoon when they got to the theater. Since Violet decided where to start shopping, she decided Lily should decide which movie, to make it fair.

"Well, let's see what's showing..." Checking the website on her phone, Lily reads over a few titles for movies and a brief summary for each. "There's one called *The Last Straw*, says it's a comedy about a ground war between two churches across the street from each other, that might be funny. There's another called *Letters from a Life Long Past*, a Romance about a soldier who wrote letters to his wife who he left at home when he went to war, I guess he dies at war and the letters were delivered to his wife after the war ended. A third contender, it's called *The Tapping at Your Window*, sounds creepy. It's a horror about a serial killer who would set up one of those water drinking bird toys outside peoples' windows that he was coming for. Not sure about you, but I don't have a tree at my window, I wouldn't mind that one."

"I don't have a tree outside my window, but I have a little brother with the internet, and it can have the same effect. I think that romance sounds pretty good, what do you think?"

"If you're ready to cry maybe. I'm more in the mood to laugh today, so how about the ground war?"

"I can live with that."

And so they watched *The Last Straw*. A Mormon church and a Christian church had been built across the street from each other, and there were constant disputes between the two heads of faith. There were aggressive exchanging of offerings between the two, furious baptism water wars and the constant one-upmanship of kindness between the two congregations. The movie did its job, they were still laughing when they left the theater.

It was days like these that Violet cherished, the ones that she could look back on when she was older and remember all the fun they had had, all the good memories of companionship. She wondered if Lily felt the same way. They had slowly began to drift apart; they didn't get as much time to talk most days. School had reached its crucial point in the year, and they had to kick it in to overdrive to be ready for their tests and hadn't been able to maintain their social lives as much. She hoped they would still be friends at College or University, even if they took different paths.

Lilian let out a long sigh after they had finished laughing, "Well, I should head home now, I told my mom I'd be home by nine, and its coming quick. I had fun, V. I wish we could do this more often."

"Yeah, we haven't been able to hang out as much lately, it kind of sucks, but I guess it's more important to focus on school for now."

"When the summer break starts, we won't have to worry about tests for a while. That will be a welcome feeling, the freedom of not having a schedule."

"Hopefully we can really start to get together more often then."

"That would be nice."

And with a final farewell, the two girls went their separate ways into the dimly lit night.

Chapter Three
The Walk with No End

   Soon after Violet had lost sight of Lily, she put in her earbuds and turned on her music. She set it to shuffle on her mixed playlist and kept on walking. She was thinking about how she and Lily used to hang out almost every week. She missed those days, the carefree ones when they had no reason to worry. She checked the time and saw it was quarter past nine. She was still a half hour walk from home, so she sends her Mom a text.

   "Hey Mom, I'm going to be a little late to get home, not by more than twenty minutes. See you soon!" and she puts her phone away again. Violet continued on her way home. This part of town didn't usually have many people on the streets, especially not at this time of night. There were six people besides her on the sidewalk. Violet's mother responded after a few minutes.

   "Okay, Honey. Just be safe on your way home. Your father wants you to hurry so we can watch a movie together. See you soon, Sweetie! Love you!"

   Violet pushed the pedestrian crossing button and started across the street while reading her mother's text. She only got to read up to "Your father". Earbuds in, eyes on her phone; Violet was completely oblivious to the drunk driver coming down the road. Too late to be able to stop, the car hits Violet in the street, and the driver leaves her there on the road as he drives off into the night.

Chapter Four
All a Dream?

Violet opened her eyes, once again welcomed by the sun, though she noted it was much softer on her eyes than yesterday morning. After having focused in, Violet also noted the cherry blossoms above her, swaying slowly in the gentle breeze. She could not for the life of her remember there being a place in all the city where there had been Cherry Blossom Trees. She rolled on to her side, and sees a mountain range in the distance, its snowy peaks nearly invisible against the cloudy skyline. The fog obscured the mountains so that they were barely visible from this distance. Between her and the crags lay a canopy of pink, a forest of cherry blossoms. She had never seen such a sight in her life, and was awestruck by its beauty. It reminded Violet of where her dreams took place most nights. She stood up on the hill and did a slow turn, ending again when she faced towards the mountains. Surrounding the hill on all sides were flourishing pink blossoms, as fair a shade as to almost look white from this distance.

Violet sits back down on the hill, leaning against the lone tree atop its crest, and tries to remember what had happened, and where she might be. She had remembered a light approaching from the corner of her eye, perhaps she had been hit by something? A car? She ran a quick inspection of her body, making sure she wasn't injured at all. Even before she began her search, she knew there would be nothing, for she felt no pain at the moment. But how did she end up here? "Is this heaven?" she thought to herself. None of it made sense at all. Tears started to form at the brim of her eyelids, and she fought to hold them back. Despite the beauty of her surroundings and the serenity of the scenery, she felt afraid. It scared her that she didn't recognize where she was, and she was worried about her parents; they would be freaking out because she hadn't come home that night. She remembered her phone, and jumped up looking for her purse. If she could just find her phone, she could find out where she was and call her parents. She walked two circles around the tree, searching the knee high grass, but to no avail. Leaning back against the tree in the impression she had left in the grass, Violet threw her head back with shut eyes, trying to prevent the tears from falling. If they never touched the ground, did it count as crying? She opened her eyes, and through watery eyes, she saw her purse in the tree above.

Violet pulls herself off the ground, wiping the stained tears from her eyes, smearing her finger tips with black eyeliner in doing so, and backs away to look for a branch low enough for her to reach. Thinking back on her track and field record, Violet believes she could easily climb the tree if she could manage to get a firm grip on one of the branches. She spots one about seven feet off the ground and makes a mental path from it to her purse. Violet only stands at five feet, seven inches tall, but has the tallest recorded height in high jump of her class. With a long enough run, it should be easy. Violet makes her way back to where the hill starts to make a steep crest, and stops while still on flat enough ground. She stretches her limbs and body to get warmed up, and starts her run. Eyes on the branch, Violet is just about to jump when something happens; she hears a voice that sounds like her own mind say "You can make it through this, I love you" and she falters slightly, her foot then gets caught on something, and she takes a dive into the grass. Lifting her head from the ground, Violet let's out a curse under her breath and makes an effort to stand up. Her foot won't allow it. She turns on to her back and sits up in the grass, her vision obscured by the tall grass. As she turns, she feels her ankle rubbing against something on all sides, as if she had a ball and chain, and reaches over to examine the issue. Her hand finds something damp and muddy around her ankle, yet it is solid beneath the grime. She tries to pull her leg out, but can't get her foot past it. She then tries to pry the noose from her foot, and fails in this endeavor as well. It won't budge. Fear starts to creep into her, what if she gets stuck here forever? Panicking, she starts kicking at her aggressor with her free leg while trying to pull her imprisoned leg to freedom. Her captor becomes annoyed by this, and lifts her above the grass, her hair dangling down and meeting ends with the grass as she is hanged up in the air.

Violet screams, flailing her arms, unsure what to do with them. She settles on holding her skirt between her legs with one hand and reaching for the ground with the other. After being held in the air for ten seconds, her screams forming a continuous string, broken for no more than a quarter second, a voice booms from all around her, filling her ears and forcing both her hands to her ears, the burden of holding her skirt being passed on to her legs.

The shouting silences her screams and fills her mind, "Why with the screaming! If you would have just stopped hitting me you wouldn't be in this mess in the first place!"

Violet was in such shock that she could hardly form words in her mind, her ears still rang with the last words of the unknown voice. "W-What? What do you mean hitting you? I was just trying to get my leg free from whatever this thing is that pulled me into the air!" She said, her voice trembling worse and worse the longer she spoke.

"That THING is my root, and it only picked you up because you were going to break it off." The voice thundered with a cold edge to its words.

Violet was unable to discern the origin of the voice. It had said that she was hitting its root, but Violet had never heard of a talking tree. Then again, she had never heard of roots moving anywhere but outward from the base of the tree, yet here she hangs. "C-Can you please tell it to put me down? I didn't mean to upset you."

The voice hesitated with its response, and Violet worried that they had ignored her. She was about to ask again, when she found herself falling to the ground. Hitting with a thud, Violet groaned a little while rubbing her soon to be bruised head. "That was pretty rude of you" she said through the pain of a bitten tongue.

"And kicking someone repeatedly isn't? You should be thanking me for not leaving you there."

Violet was good with neither apologies nor showing gratitude, "Who exactly am I talking to?"

"Isn't it obvious?"

"As much as it seems that I'm talking to a tree, I would sooner think I've gone insane than that a tree is actually talking to me." She responded while wiping the dirt off of her skirt and feeling her ankle.

"Well then you may want to have a checkup for your mental health, because you're actually talking to a tree."

Violet sat down in the grass, the tears were back. She struggled to hold them back. It was all too much for her to process; she was somewhere that she didn't recognize, far away from everyone she knew, and, worst of all, she was talking to a tree. She must have truly lost it. Through her sobs she heard something, a voice much too soft to be the tree, it seemed so distant yet it sounded as if it were her own thoughts. She stifled her tears to try and listen in better.

"Patient Glendale... collision... fractured ribs... arm broken... concussion... shallow breathing... comatose..." Coma. Had she actually been hit by a car? That was impossible, wasn't it? She felt fine though! Where was the voice coming from? It must be wrong!

Then she heard crying, and all the emotions came back to her as a wave. She wept with the ownerless tears

Chapter Five
The Doctor's Report

Diana couldn't stop thinking of her daughter. Where was she? It was half past ten, she wasn't picking up her phone, and she hadn't come home yet. She was riddled with worry and anger. She so badly needed to hear from her baby, to know she was ok. But at the same time, she was so grounded when she got back. However, no matter how much she consoled herself and her husband reassured her that "She's just being a teenager", Diana couldn't shake this feeling that something was wrong. That was when they got the call.

The phone rang in the kitchen and Diana went to answer it. Before she picked it up, a wave of fear washed over her. It was the hospital. With trembling hands, she answered the call and raised the phone to her ear.

"Hello?"

"Hello, Mrs. Glendale?" It was the secretary Nina

Her heart dropped. "Y-Yes, this is her."

"I'm sorry to be the one to tell you, but I'm afraid your daughter was brought in by ambulance in critical condition. I think you should come down and see."

Alarms were going off in her head, she couldn't keep a constant train of thought. "O-. Okay, we will be down as soon as we can. T-Thank you, Nina." She could barely keep herself together before she hung up, the last words barely audible. "Bryan, you need to come here, now. Bring Peter too."

They left for the hospital immediately.

***

The whole ride there, Peter was asking questions that his parents either didn't have the information to answer or couldn't bring themselves to answer. Despite the short actuality of the drive, it was the longest that

Diana had ever taken. Once they arrived, without hesitation, they ran through the main doors to the front desk with one goal: to find their daughter. The nurse gave them a room number and Diana started in the direction, husband and son in tow. Once they arrived at the recovery room, Diana and Bryan told Peter to wait outside.

Violet was laying on a bed that stood three feet off of the ground in a room that was almost entirely white. The only distinct colors in the room were the lines on the heart rate monitor, Violet's golden hair, and the bloody bandage around her forehead. Her parents approached the bed with a mix of relief and concern. Relief to hear the monitor beeping in sync with Violet's heart and to see her, and concern over every other aspect of their daughter's health.

Diana leaned over the side of the bed and ran a hand down Violet's face; there were scratches in a haphazard pattern across the entirety of it. Diana leaned in and planted a kiss on her daughter's forehead. Bryan had been rubbing a comforting hand between Diana's shoulders the whole time. Diana backed away, staying close enough to hold Violet's hand, while Bryan moved closer. He brushed some hair out of her face and tucked it behind her ear, then whispered into it "You can make it through this, I love you." He backed away after placing a kiss on the same spot that Diana had left hers.

The doctor entered the room as Bryan backed away. Diana recognized him immediately, it was Doctor Lindbel. He was known among the staff for having the best record of patient survival and recovery. He was also assigned to the most critical patients. "Hello, Diana, Bryan. I saw your son outside, I assured him it's going to be ok."

"How is she? Is she going to be ok?" Diana was too worried for pleasantries, she needed to know her daughter would be ok.

"I'll start from the top. Patient Violet Glendale, delivered by an ambulance that was called in by a citizen who happened to be passing by when she was hit in a single car collision, presumably a drunk driver. She has been checked over and this is what we've found: she has three fractured ribs on the right side of her ribcage, her right arm has been broken by the force of the blow, she has a concussion, most likely from when she fell to the ground, she had been found to have shallow breathing, it's possibly a bruised lung, but the only thing worth worrying about is that she was recovered from the collision scene in a comatose state. It's truly a miracle, much worse could have happened, I'm sure you could imagine how. She is going in for surgery early tomorrow morning to set her arm back into place and get it in a cast. If she does have a bruised lung, we plan to find out during the operation tomorrow as well, if that's the case, she may have a minor breathing issue even after she is awake, but chances are it will heal up quickly. The concussion is nothing serious while she is asleep, she would be very drowsy almost all the time and her balance and coordination would be askew while awake. However, a coma is very serious, with good luck she could wake up tomorrow, worst case she may not wake up for a very long time... if at all. While it may not seem that way right now, she is a very lucky girl."

Diana tried to soothe her mind with the doctor's words, but she could not shake her worry. Diana and Bryan talked it all over with Doctor Lindbel and were eventually, while not worry free, able to calm themselves down to a functional state. Diana refused to go home, she was adamant on staying the night with her daughter to make sure she was okay. She sent Bryan home with Peter and settled in for the night in the armchair beside Violet's bed, wrapping herself in the blanket that the hospital had provided for her, leaving an arm free to comfort her unresponsive Violet, while she wept for her.

Chapter Six
The Terms of a Tree

Violet awoke on the hill, her eyes outlined in red and raw from crying. This marked the fifth time she had woken up in the night, and she decided to make it the last until tomorrow. She sat up against the lone tree, yawning, and stretched her arms out. There were no dreams that night; instead they were nightmares, and they would not permit rest. The sun was only just starting to peek over the mountains tops, staining the sky with a purple more beautiful than any shade Violet had ever seen; it was deep yet soft and still speckled with blazing white dots, like a tapestry made by a god.

Above her, the tree's canopy rustled with the wind, pink flowers falling slowly onto Violet's lap. She picked up one of the blossoms, it was still wet with dew. The dew only made it more beautiful. Raising it to her nose, it smelt of fruit, so strong that it made Violet begin to salivate. However, Violet had no thirst to quench and no hunger to sate, wherever she was, she did not have to meet the basic needs to live. She had slept, not to satisfy a tired body, but to try and find comfort and reprieve from one nightmare, but only found more worry caused by the next.

Violet stood up and stretched again. She had been able to reason enough with the tree that it would let her sleep underneath its canopy. Before she had settled in to sleep the evening past, the tree had formally introduced itself as "Tok-Nulon" and had welcomed her officially to The Dreamscape, and, before she could introduce herself, she had fallen asleep. It had taken much deliberation for her to be allowed to stay on the hill, but in addition to letting her sleep beneath the tree, she had convinced him to drop her purse down. Tok-Nulon had explained to Violet that the trees of this forest did not speak, but conveyed thoughts to one another through telepathy. This opened the possibility for them to speak to anything or nothing; however they willed it to be. Finally, when it was late into the night, she had come to an agreement with the trees;

she could stay the night under Tok-Nulon's cover, under the condition that she would take no action against the trees of this forest during her stay; if she was to provoke them by any means, she was at their mercy.

Violet remembered her warm welcome yesterday and had no desire to reenact it today, or ever again, so these terms were easy for her to abide by.

"You rise before the sun, little one. What is it that troubles you so?" Violet had not shared the specifics with Tok-Nulon of how she had ended up here.

"I don't belong here, I should be at home with my family." Violet could feel a knot forming in her stomach and her throat began to constrict, making it difficult to speak.

"You belong where you wish to feel accepted. Someday everyone must part with their creators, perhaps now is your time. You have seen the mountains to the south, yes? I have faint memories of soaring over them when I was but a seed. There were many of us that crossed over them that year. I was the only one to land on this hill, as is apparent. On the other side of the range lies another forest, not as great in size as the one you see now, for it borders an ocean. Any who are unlucky enough to be carried over the ocean are never heard from again; the distance is too great to reach land and lay your roots. This is where I belong, not because I landed here, but because I have made this my home."

Violet knew she did not belong here, and his consoling did not help, "Is there anything in the forest? If I travel to that lake, is there anything I should know to watch out for?" Perhaps she could find a way to wake herself up, if she was asleep that was, and not just... somewhere up above.

"Dangers lay in this forest the same as any other. However, there is a rumor among the trees towards the lake of a Manticore prowling near the water's eastern border. You should be prepared to run rather than hide. If the rumor is true, it would be wise to note its heightened sense of smell and its poor sight. It is especially quick on foot, however, in a forest it struggles to weave between obstacles. Do not travel in a straight line or it will catch you with ease."

Violet listened to this with a slightly open mouth, squinting at the tree. She had assumed to hear something like "Watch out for wolves" or "Keep an eye out for pits", not "There's a Manticore near there". She didn't even know what a Manticore was, so how was she supposed to know what to watch for? "Yeah, okay. I'll, um, I'll keep an eye out for it. Thanks for the warning." Violet said with as much authenticity as she could fake.

"Little one, you have not introduced yourself. The other trees wish to know how they should address you if you pass by them."

Violet faced Tok-Nulon, her skirt swaying in the wind. "My name is Violet Glendale." She says, unsure where to focus her gaze on the tree.

"Glendale... the trees will do what we can to help if the need arises. Go now, find where you belong."

With that, Violet turned towards the lake and began her descent. The hill was rather steep, she struggled to keep herself from breaking into an unintentional sprint; each step a clumsy drop, as if she were running down a flight of stairs where each step stood a foot higher than the last. Each step brought new ground that was gradually becoming more flat as she went. Finally, three steps from the base, her foot caught on a rock and she tumbled down the remaining distance. Raising from the ground, Violet felt the dirt under her fingernails and the throbbing pain of her stubbed toe. She felt a lot more embarrassed by the little things now that she knew the trees bore witness to them. Damn rocks! She was positive that everything in her dream world had a will of its own, and she had no intention of making any enemies out of them, no matter how inanimate things looked. For now her thoughts would be kept to herself.

"You can't blame the rock for your clumsiness, Glendale." A voice she hadn't heard before, it was more feminine than that of Tok-Nulon.

Violet felt the red gathering in her cheeks, not only had the trees seen, they had also heard. If they had heard, the rock might have also.

"Rocks aren't living silly; they can't hear thoughts like us." A second new voice, deeper than the last. It was too much for her. Violet felt so embarrassed by something that should have rightfully had no witnesses. This new world made her feel so awkward!

"Don't blame anyone else for your not being able to keep your thoughts to yourself." Three! Three trees had seen her trip on a rock! She brought her knees up to her chin and hid her face in the folds of her skirt.

"More than three saw that mishap," she heard from what sounded like the entirety of New York at once.

Violet did her best not to think. Until she knew how to keep her mind to herself she couldn't even trust her own thoughts. What a strange world this was.

Chapter Seven
Quiet Company

Diana had become so used to seeing families crying over loved ones in the hospital she worked at; she had never thought she would be in their situation. They had taken her daughter in for surgery that morning and when she had been returned there was a cast around her right arm. Bryan had brought Diana her book while Violet was in surgery.

"I wish I could stay to see her, but Peter is home alone. He was still asleep when I left, so he will be wondering where I am if he wakes up before I'm back." Raising Diana out of the chair, Bryan hugs his wife, running a hand along her back, and whispering in her ear, "She's a tough girl, she'll make it through this, D." With a farewell kiss, Bryan leaves the hospital room.

Diana hadn't read a page yet, she was engrossed with the wellbeing of her daughter. Even though it was completely out of her power, Diana so badly wished she could help her somehow. The best she could do was to stay by her side, and so that is what she did.

Diana would whisper to Violet, reminiscing about when she was just a baby, about how cute she was. She talked about the silly things that she did as she grew up, like when Diana and Bryan had found her in the kitchen in a puddle of whipped cream at three years old, the empty canister beside her and the guilt splattered across her face in the form of white puffs of sugar, or when Diana was teaching Violet how to drive two years ago, after she had gotten her learners. She was always so touchy on the brakes, she nearly gave them both whiplash at every stop sign. Diana had made herself laugh with these memories, and could only hope that Violet had heard as well.

The next day, Diana had begun reading her book to Violet, restarting from the beginning so she got the whole story too. It was called *Morning Love Notes*. It talked about the different things that a husband would do for his wife since they rarely got to spend time together anymore. Their work hours were opposite each other, so when one of them got home to sleep, the other would just be getting up for work. He would leave notes around the house for his wife to find when she got up in the mornings, saying different things like "Have a good day at work honey!" or chain messages of up to nine notes that together would recount a moment during their dating period when they both had a wonderful time. He would rekindle those moments to remind them both why they love each other. The story warmed Diana's heart when she read it and made her glad that she and Bryan got to spend time together and still enjoyed each other's company after so long.

Occasionally a doctor or nurse would come to check up on Violet; make sure her IV drop was still full and make sure everything was still running properly, then return to the hallway, leaving Diana alone with her daughter once more. Things continued this way for a week. Bryan and Peter would visit every other day for a couple hours, and Diana had begun to sleep throughout the day to pass the time, though she did not sleep well. There would be slight irregularities in Violet's heart monitor now and then, but they proved to be nothing. Today, however, coming to the end of May, the heart rate monitor began beeping at over twice the regular speed and it would not return to its normal pace.

Chapter Eight

The Lake

Violet's voyage to the lake had taken her longer than anticipated. From the hill it did not appear to be this far away. In a complete perimeter of the lake were cherry blossom trees, and what passed for a beach was littered with their pink blossoms. Violet had mostly avoided further embarrassments, though she had been attacked by a fuzzy creature resembling a chipmunk who had tried to steal some of her hair. The trees had found this especially humorous. Arriving at the beach was the greatest relief Violet had experienced in her dream world so far. The walk here had taken two days and two nights. The beach, however, was not sand like Violet was used to; it consisted of a fine gravel, not sharp enough to cause harm. She felt filthy, her clothes were beginning to stick to her skin and her hair was becoming matted. She had no change of clothes with her, so she decided to try and wash her clothes in the lake. She had only ever washed her clothes with one of the laundry machines at home, but her discomfort was enough incentive for her to learn without it. Stripping down on the lake shore, her shirt peeling away from her skin like tape, Violet finds a large black rock on the beach, close enough to the lake to sit on and reach the water.

The rock is warm on Violet's legs and brings a comfort she had yet to experience in this new world. Beginning with her undergarments, Violet sets her clothes into the water and rubs away mud and grime with her thumb, dipping them into the water frequently to keep them wet, making slow progress. Violet doesn't feel comfortable with the idea of living trees seeing her naked, and tries to block out the idea of there being anything but her, the rock, her clothes and the water. As Violet finished washing each article, she would lay them out to dry from the sun and the rock's warmth. Once her clothes had all been cleaned, Violet put herself into the water to wash the dirt from her skin and from beneath her nails, bringing the comb she had found in her purse as well.

The surface of the water was a serene sight, pink blossoms were scattered across it and the only ripples came from Violet. The water itself was a deep blue, eyes unable to pierce far below the surface.

Violet sat in the water after having combed her hair; it was warmer than the rock had been. She looked around the lake; at the far end, across from where she swam, she saw a pair of deer-like animals drinking from the lake. She couldn't make out much detail from this distance, but one of them had large antlers while the other was bare headed, and they both looked to have what looked like scales across their hind legs. In the distance she heard the sharp cry of birds as a small group of crows took to the skies near the deer. The pair of deer raised their heads from the water and looked in the direction of the birds. Not more than a second later they turned to run before the horned one was crushed by the paw of a lion; its mate continued fleeing into the forest. This was no ordinary lion. Its head and body were that of a lion, but its fur was green with a black tinge to it, it had the hind legs of a goat, and it had the tail of a scorpion. Violet lowered herself into the water, she remembered seeing a picture of this. At the time when Tok-Nulon had explained it to her, Violet did not remember, but after having seen it once more, she remembered this creature from one of her brother's books. This was indeed a Manticore. The beast dragged its kill into the shade of the trees, away from the lake.

Violet was frozen with fear, the water did not seem so warm anymore. Slowly, Violet made her way to the shore again, staying concealed beneath the water's surface for as long as possible. Upon arriving at the shore, Violet tries as quietly as possible to lift herself out of the water, afraid that the noise would catch the Manticore's attention. Against her instincts, Violet puts on her dry clothes while the water still runs down her skin. After replacing her comb in her purse, Violet's fear gets the better of her and she runs into the forest. Before she can get to the cover of the tree line, she hears a roar from across the lake. Whirling around, Violet sees the Manticore with a blood soaked maw staring at her with piercing, crimson eyes. Before Violet can turn to run, it is gone into the trees. She flees in the other direction in a panic, her mind full of questions. "Can I die in a dream? Will I just wake up if I die? But is that a risk I'm willing to take?" All these thoughts and many more were racing through her mind. From her past experiences with dreams, anytime that she was about to die in a dream, she would always wake up. That risk didn't seem to be worth taking this time though.

***

Doctor Lindbel and his assistant nurse were at a loss; they went over the possibilities, and all seemed unlikely. They ran various tests that were unlikely but possible, and still nothing. There seemed to be nothing they could do. They had sent Diana into the hallway with nothing but her worry. Meanwhile, the girl in the bed was fighting a battle they could do nothing to aid in.

***

Violet did not know how long she had been running for. After the Manticore had left in pursuit, she took flight in the opposite direction around the lake. Occasionally a roar would sound out behind her from a fair distance, slowly getting closer. Eventually she would be caught; she had to think of something.

All of the trees near Violet were constantly reminding her of Tok-Nulon's guidance. "It has your scent, keep running and find something to mask your scent with," they would advise her, along with a plethora of other recommendations. She had no room for her own thoughts through their cascade of overlapping messages.

"You cannot escape," a new voice in her mind said. The trees had fallen silent. This new voice was sleek like the night and bore a tone of underlying death. It gave her the mental image of a cat talking to a mouse under its paws. "You were a fool to leave such a distinct scent on your clothes. I have never smelt something so peculiar before, and I will not forget it. The rock you had been near reeks of it. A shame, really."

What scent? Violet had just washed herself and her clothes, she didn't remember them smelling anything short of normal! Wait! Her perfume! She had a bottle of it in her purse, that must be what the

Manticore smells! Violet went rummaging through her purse as best she could while keeping her pace. She finds her perfume bottle tucked away in a zipper near the back of her purse. She smells the nozzle, not daring to spray her skin lest the scent stays on her. It smelled of jasmine, a very strong smell indeed. If this Manticore had the sense of smell that its feline head implied, there was no doubt it would be able to smell such an intoxicating fragrance even from this distance. Taking her perfume bottle in her hand, she hurls it as far as she can in the direction opposite the lake and continues running away from it, praying it didn't get caught by the canopy above.

"Changing directions will not save you now that I know your scent." A cold sweat had started to form on Violet's neck, the beast either knew she had turned, or it had changed course to pursue the bottle. Violet could not risk turning to look, the fear was too great for her to manage anything now except to run. Her legs were practically moving on their own. "Why do you sit still? Have you given up, frail one?" The Manticore had taken the bait! "You are near, I can smell it." Violet did not stop, the Manticore would soon find the broken glass and continue its search. Hopefully by then Violet could make enough ground on it that it would not be able to find her.

"Very quick thinking Glendale. The trees are with you, but we can do little to stop a beast of such ferocity, it would tear out our roots were we to try and slow it."

Violet did her best to ignore them, if at the very least to not answer them in her thoughts. She did not want to run the risk of the Manticore having the same psychic powers as the trees. She ran for the remainder of the day, and long into the night. Her legs did not tire, for she did not need rest in this strange world. She did not hear from the Manticore again, and only slowed her pace after having been reassured by the trees countless times.

***

Doctor Lindbel had never seen anything like it, one minute the heart rate monitor was an incessant whir, the next it had been restored to its regular pace without explanation. They called Diana back into the room. Her eyes were red and her cheeks stained. They informed her of what had happened. The doctors reviewed the peculiar case amongst themselves later. They had no idea what had happened and could only pray it wouldn't come about once more.

Chapter Nine
Night in the Dreamscape

The night was silent, broken only by a foreign chirping in the distance. Violet did not recognize this noise, it was not that of a cricket nor that of a bird she knew. The stars overhead were dazzling, white beacons in a dark night. Among them was a certain group of stars that, to Violet, looked as if they were following her. She checked on them now and then, and they looked to be constantly moving towards her. She felt out of place in this world, she felt awkward from always being watched, even if it was just by trees. She had been kept company by various trees that introduced themselves to her, the most recent was a cherry blossom that was still young by the standards of this forest, and its name was Kuh-Gothak. It was the latest, but not the only one, to also warn Violet of The Gazer; she had caught his attention they said. When she asked who The Gazer was, no one would answer, saying only that he acts as the peacekeeper between all factions of the Dreamscape. He was recognized as the omnipotent entity of their world. The trees spoke in reverence of his name.

Violet walked without an objective. She had no understanding of this world, she did not fully understand why she was here, and she did not know how to return home. Perhaps this Gazer could help her. If he was the strongest thing in this world, couldn't he take her home? She continued aimlessly through the night.

"You approach the grove of Heidskun, little one." Kuh-Gothak said. "The queen of Nymphs resides within. She knows of your nearing, and invites you in."

Violet knew what a nymph was, remembering it from one of her brother's books as well. It appealed to her much more than a Manticore. Violet oddly found herself a little giddy to meet this Queen of nymphs, despite having only just learnt of her. "How far away is this grove?" Violet asked the surrounding trees.

"You have already entered its boundaries, child," answered the voice of a woman. "Continue forward and you shall find my abode."

Violet began to notice different trees ahead, the cherry blossoms grew sparse and were instead replaced with green foliage. The canopy overhead began to grow thick with green leaves, blocking out the stars and the night sky. As Violet continued onward the trees came closer and closer together. She had to start going around certain groups that were blocking the path and in between others. Their bark was a greyish black and had distinct ridges across its surface with deep grooves between. It was rough on her skin, often leaving white scratch marks across it, and threatening to tear at her clothes. Once more, the canopy began to change. The leaves were replaced with the long strands of a weeping willow. Violet recognized these trees, they had always stood out to her with their distinct type of foliage that hung low in long leaves. The trees grew further apart once more and the canopy became less dense, the stars starting to become visible once more. Through the canopy, Violet could not believe what she was seeing. A giant tree stood in the distance ahead of her, nearly four times the height of the willows with branches reaching great distances out from the trunk. Its canopy reached past the longest of its branches and was bustling with life. Fireflies all around the magnificent tree lit up the trunk with nests hanging from various branches and lit up the canopy as well, its vibrant green visible from afar. Violet dreaded to think of how much homework could be made out of such a beautiful thing, and wished she had seen this from the hill. She was sure she would have if the fog had not been hanging that day.

"That is the mother tree, little one." An elderly sounding voice told her. "It has stood longer than any of us on this side of the mountain range."

Violet grew excited, she wanted to see what lived within its canopy and around its base. She started to run, growing ever nearer to the greatwood. In the distance she saw its trunk at ground level. As she approached it, Violet bore witness to the beauty beneath its canopy. Around the trees base were numerous ponds that glowed yellow with firofly light, illuminating the water and revealing the sprites hovering

~ 30 ~

above its surface. A huge open meadow lay behind the tree. The ground became marshy as she walked towards the great tree's base. Violet noticed that all of the sprites and Fairies were watching her.

"Welcome to the haven of Heidskun, young one. Your kind has not been here in a very long time." Violet heard the voice before she saw its owner, and recognized it as the woman's voice from before. Returning her eyes to the base of the tree, there now stood a tall woman with long green hair and skin so white that the light of the fireflies made her glow. She wore a dress that looked to be made of moss and was woven with wildflowers. "Will you come with me into the mother tree? I would very much like to talk with you if you would grant me your time."

Violet was at a loss for words. This woman spoke so elegantly and looked so beautiful while holding herself with such pride that Violet felt ashamed with her own etiquette and attire. "Um, I-." Words failed her.

"It's okay if you cannot speak. I know what it is that you would like to say. You are not hiding your thoughts very well, my girl." She said with a smile and a slight tilt of her head. "I appreciate how you think of me. Would you like to come in now?" she asked, her eyes looking at Violet hopefully.

Violet saw no reason to decline. She nodded, having still been tongue tied, even more so due to her new found embarrassment, and followed the Queen into the tree.

Chapter Ten
Sanctuary

The inside of the tree was illuminated by the light of the fireflies. The tree was hollow, to Violet's surprise. Around the interior walls of the tree there was a walkway carved from the wood into steps. The greatwood looked substantially larger from the inside. Looking up, Violet could not distinguish the ceiling from the walkways as they grew nearer together in the distance. Centered in the base of the tree was a pool of clear water encircled by a wall of stones. The stones were being held together by a grey and gold substance that looked wet. Holes had been dug throughout the base of the tree that were filled with various wildflowers and shrubs in different arrangements. Vines crawled upward along the walls of the trunk as far as the eye could see. Rooms had been carved into the walls at various heights along the walkway, some had beds and some had baths.

"Would you like to see where you will be staying?" The woman asked.

Violet was able to gather her thoughts enough to respond with a simple "Sure" and followed the Nymph lady up the walkway.

"I believe that you will like it very much here. Hestaphal will be making an appearance tonight at the gala being held by the sprites; I think you might like to meet him."

Violet was surprised with the woman's kindness; they had only just met, Violet being a foreign visitor, and she was inviting her to festivities and offering hospitality before Violet even asked a question out loud. Violet tried her hardest to convince herself it was not suspicious, fearing that everyone could read her thoughts and would be offended.

"This will be your room during your stay. Feel free to use anything that you find within. If you would like to bathe, the room beyond that door is free for your own personal use. There is a change of clothes in the dresser if you would like to. Please do make yourself at home. I will be back later on to part for the festival, if you would like to join me then." And with that the Queen ascended the stairs further, leaving Violet to inspect her room alone.

Violet entered into the doorway that was covered by a thick black curtain. Inside the bedroom, white silken curtains covered a window on the far wall hanging from a bar that adorned a rose shaped stud on each end, so that the curtains could not fall off. A closet and dresser were to the left on the same wall as the entrance, hand carved out of oak and patterned with grooves and shapes. Violet was most fond of the bed. It was a queen size canopy bed carved from a dark wood, its curtains were white with spacing between the threads enough to see through up close but to look as a solid color from afar. The curtains hung from wooden bars that had been carved with lines that reminded Violet of waves on the ocean. There were three bars protruding from each column of the bed that connected them to their three look-a-likes. The columns had grooves carved into them that made Violet think of Tiki totems. Violet approached the bed to inspect the bedding. There were white square cushions with golden embroidery around the edges and forming leaves across the surface. A white pillow sat surrounded by the cushions that wore a simplistic white cover with grey ovals in a haphazard arrangement. The blanket felt heavy to Violet, she assumed it to be a down filled one. It was inside a grey sheet that fit it perfectly. Testing the bed, Violet sank into its mattress. She felt like never getting up.

Violet surveyed the remainder of the room from her new destination. In the corner opposite the bed there was a mirror that spanned from floor to ceiling. Violet felt the urge to see her reflection, she felt a bit dirty after her journey here. Standing in front of the mirror, Violet was greeted by her reflection. Her face had a couple scratches and her arms had faint white lines across them; nothing serious. Her skirt had a cut in it though and her shirt was starting to get balls of fabric building up. This upset Violet; she had worn her favorite clothing when she went to the mall with Lily, and now they were getting ruined. Violet walked over to the dresser and looked through the drawers. In the middle left one she found a gown that, when held up to her, barely dragged across the floor. Looking at the mirror with the gown to her body, Violet admires it. The gown is a light blue. It splits at the stomach making a V shape up to and around the collar bone and a reverse V towards the ground. Within the cut of the V there is a white dress sewn onto the blue gown. Beneath the gown in the dresser, there was a towel. Violet picks up the towel and brings it with the dress and her towards the washroom.

Violet finds herself hesitant to use the bath, for the doorways are without a door. Her bedroom had only the black curtain for privacy, and the bathroom had even less; its own curtain was white and nearly transparent due to the size of the holes between its threads. Eventually, Violet convinces herself that her need to be clean is greater than the risk of being seen. The water is warm. The sound of songbirds enters through the window and makes the time fly by. She wonders how these people could have running water in a tree. She remembered hearing from one of her science classes that plants had something like veins, like her own that carry blood, but that the plants' carry water and sugar to keep it alive. Is that how they did it? Tapping into the veins of the tree? But that would kill the tree, she thought, and this one was very much alive. She was also puzzled by how the tree was alive despite being hollowed out. Violet spends a whole hour submerged, only deciding to leave once it starts to feel cold. With shriveled hands, Violet lifts herself out of the bath and reaches for her towel. The moment her hand finds the towel, there is a knock at the entrance to her bedroom. Ripping the towel out from beneath the gown, Violet fumbles with it until it unravels, long enough to cover her body, and holds it in front of her, only having enough time to get it in place before a young boy with Elfin ears and blond hair holding a stack of towels appears at the door to the bathroom, his face instantly becoming a tomato. The boy took a sharp gasp before a shoe hit him square between the eyes. Violet screamed at him to get out.

"I- I'm sorry miss!" The boy turns on a dime but finds he is unable to move away from the door. "I thought the room was empty when no one answered!" The boy managed to mutter, clearly flustered, before Violet threw the next closest thing to her at him with all her force. Her second shoe hit him in the back of the head, almost making him fall over.

"Why did you come in if no one answered?! Why didn't you just leave it outside?!" Violet was more embarrassed then she had ever remembered feeling. Grabbing the dress, she runs out of view of the door, her bare back starting to chill from the water still running down it and her wet hair hanging against it.

"I'm sorry miss! I was told to come and change the towels out! When you didn't answer I thought I would just come and change them and leave! I'm sorry, I didn't mean to peek at you!"

"Why are you still here, idiot!?" Violet was hiding in the shower, its stone wall blocking vision from the door. She dried herself hurriedly, her face still red with a mix of embarrassment and anger. How could he be so stupid? Why hadn't he left yet? Soon after, four towels came flying into the room making the curtain sail into the room. With one final apology, the boy left the bedroom.

Violet put on the dress in the shower, still unwilling to leave it. She sat in the shower for a while longer thinking about the boy. She thought he was cute, and was angry with herself for thinking it. Finally, she decided to go to the mirror; her curiosity over the dress getting the better of her. Once in front of the mirror, Violet was even more pleased with it than before. Its blue fabric complimented her eyes nicely and her blond hair seemed almost golden against the white interior of the gown. She liked how it caressed her figure, but was annoyed with having to lift it slightly to keep it from dragging across the floor. Violet went and laid on the bed, sinking into it once more. She ended up falling asleep, for how long she, did not know. She was woken up by the Queen when the windows were still devoid of sunlight.

"The festivities will soon begin, young one. Would you give me your company for the walk down?"

Violet was still afflicted with the drowsiness of sleep. She answered with a nod and brought herself off of the bed.

"Splendid. It has been a long time since Hestaphal came to visit; your presence here coincided with a very rare occasion. That dress looks wonderful on you, dear."

"You think so? I really like it too." Violet answered, the grogginess starting to fade from her.

"Perhaps you may take it with you when you leave. Oh, how rude of me; I do not believe I've introduced myself properly. My name is Diana, I am the Queen of the Nymphs."

Chapter Eleven
Festival of Bells

Violet was confused. Was it just a coincidence that the Nymph Queen had the same name as her mother? They descended the stairs slowly; the cheers of partygoers becoming increasingly louder. Arriving at the base, the pair approached the door to the courtyard, the full force of the noise blocked only by the entrance door. As they opened the door to the outside, the festivals sound flooded the tree.

The courtyard of Heidskun was full of life. There were Elves in all manners of clothing; some of the men were flirting with a group of tall women with green hair and wore earthen robes that parted on one side of their legs, revealing their bright, white skin underneath. Most of the women Elves had spread out and struck up conversations with the various other attendees. Swarms of Fairies wearing various dresses and garbs made of different types of foliage were playing games in the air, throwing magic spears made of dust at each other in mock javelin wars and darting around in games of tag. Short bearded men, that Violet could only assume were Dwarves, were spread out across the courtyard in clusters carrying frothing mugs and visiting with the various other guests. And in the ponds were men and women with the bottom halves of fish, they were not only Mermaids, however, for Violet could also see goat horns protruding from some of their heads just slightly above and behind their ears, as well as hair coating the upper half of their bodies. Among all of this, two things stood out most to Violet; in the sky there flew a Phoenix; it glowed a bright yellow with red tinges at the tips of its wings and searing white eyes. Its light resembled that of the sun. The second thing that held Violet's attention was a Unicorn in the meadows behind the tree where the main festivities were being held. Violet was spellbound by the majestic beast, its fur was a white so pure and bright that it was almost blinding, and its horn whiter yet with spiral grooves that climbed the horn and met at its tip. The Unicorn's eyes were purple, and its mane was a shimmering silver that shone in the light of the Phoenix.

The Nymph Queen took Violet's hand, leading her in the direction one of the ponds. "I would like you to meet the Capricorns. They may appear off-putting to you now, but if you get to know them you will find they are a very unique group of people." Once at the ponds, Diana introduced Violet to the Capricorns as "the Human who outsmarted the Manticore of the lake." This appeared to interest the Capricorns, for they would not stop asking Violet questions about it for quite a long time.

"Did you hear his voice in your head?" "How did you outsmart him?" "Was he upset when he found out?" "Did you tease him about getting away?" and Violet answered the questions rather plainly.

Some of the Capricorns began to yawn. "She doesn't know how to make a story interesting, does she?"

"It sure seems that way, doesn't it?"

"Why don't you tell it again? But try and make it more exciting this time!"

"Yeah! Really make it sound heroic this time! Like you taunted it, calling it dumb and that kind of thing!"

Violet could tell what the Nymph Queen had meant; they were like children, wanting stuff to be exciting and to be entertained. They were exhausting. At the edge of the pool behind the Capricorns stood the Nymph Queen, covering her mouth with her sleeve. Violet could tell she was grinning by the way her eyes were shaped. Violet felt a twinge of frustration, was Diana playing a joke on her? Violet did not like talking in front of groups, it made her very nervous, especially when she didn't know any of the people she was talking to. Violet managed to persuade the Capricorns that she was out of time; the Nymph Queen needed her to keep their schedule. The Capricorns did not seem upset after Violet had told them she had to go, they waved goodbye with enthusiasm and continued to say goodbye until Violet was well out of ear shot, even for their shouting.

"Did you know they were going to ask me so many questions?" Violet demanded to know.

Diana was suppressing a laugh when she answered, "Of course not, my girl. I just thought you would like to meet them. Why, did you not enjoy talking to them?"

"Enjoy? I'm not good with talking to people I don't know, you should have caught that when we met!"

"Oh, don't worry about it. People find it cute when a girl like you gets a bit tongue tied." She said, nudging Violet with her elbow. Diana was leading them towards the tents where the Unicorn was wandering among the revelers. "So, how are you enjoying the Festival of Bells so far?"

"I don't understand why it's called the Festival of *Bells*, I haven't seen or heard a single bell."

"You will understand as the night goes on."

Diana stopped near a group of revelers to join the conversation. They were mostly Elves with the exception of a couple Dwarves. Among the Elves was a young boy with blond hair. Violet and the boy made eye contact, and Violet turned to hide her quickly reddening face. The boy was looking down at his shoes in an attempt to hide his own flushed face. The conversation stopped abruptly as the adults noticed both of the kids hiding. Taking quick glances between the two, and noticing the bits of red not well hidden, the adults, except for Diana, exchanged a few grins before one of the Dwarves started again.

"Oi lad, that the lass you walked in on?" the Dwarf had a red nose from drinking too much and his green eyes narrowed as his grin widened, revealing yellow teeth. "She's quite a looker, ain't she? Can't blame you for stealing a peek."

One of the Elf women slapped the Dwarf. "That is very rude of you to speak like that, Gein."

Violet was mortified; the boy had told other people about what had happened. She could feel her face getting hot with the blood that lit her cheeks up like fire.

"Sorry, but ye can't deny her stunning *features*." He said, nudging the boy with his elbow before letting out a loud guttural laugh.

"Come Violet, the festival will soon begin in full." Diana took

Violet towards the tents with a glare at Gein and a beckoning finger to the boy. Reluctantly, the young Elf followed.

Violet was nudging Diana, trying to get her attention. Why had she brought the boy? Violet did not think this night could get any worse.

Diana ignored the elbow in her side. Once they were further down the hill, Diana turned to the boy. "What's your name?" Her voice was stern.

"Taivna, ma'am."

"And what is this about you 'stealing a peek', Taivna?"

"I told her I was sorry! Gein was just trying to get me in trouble!"

"I don't want excuses, I want to know what happened." Her emerald eyes were giving the boy an icy stare.

"Tyvald is one of the housekeepers for the mother tree, he is the tallest one in the group you found me with. He told me to bring some towels up to her room because he said that she wasn't there at the moment. When I got there I knocked and no one answered. I figured I could just drop them off and go before anyone knew, so I went to bring the towels to the bathroom but when I got to the doorway, well..."

"Well, what?"

Reliving the moment made Violet feel even more awkward than she already was. "Don't make him answer, please." Violet said, her voice but a whisper. Neither of the others heard her.

"She had just gotten out of the bath, and well... She had a towel up so I didn't see anything, but I couldn't hardly move, I was caught completely off guard. I didn't think anyone was there! I'm sorry!" The boy had dropped to his knees, his forehead to the earth. Perhaps, Violet thought, he had been just as embarrassed as she had been.

Diana turned to Violet. "Is this true?"

"Yes" Violet responded feebly.

Diana turned to the boy, "You may go, but tell Tyvald that I will be talking to him later."

"Th-Thank you madam." The boy was surprised for having gotten off so easily. He jumped off the ground. "I'm truly sorry, I di-"

"Go now, you've caused this girl enough embarrassment, no need to make her blush more." Diana's expression had softened. Once the boy had gone back up the hill, Diana turned back to Violet. "I told them all not to bother you for now, but I suppose Tyvald wanted to get a story from the boy." Diana sat down beside Violet on the hill. Brushing hair out of Violet's eyes, Diana continues. "It could have been worse. For instance, if I hadn't left a towel under the dress for you." She said with a soft chuckle. Violet was slowly lifting her head from between her knees. "The night is not yet over, little one. Come, let me introduce you to Hestaphal." Diana lifts herself from the hill, offering a hand to Violet. Violet was comforted by how similar Diana was to her mother. Taking Diana's hand, Violet stands up once more, and the two continue towards the tents and the Unicorn.

"He likes you. Can you tell?"

"Don't say that!" Violet's face was red once more.

***

It was night, and the hospital was relatively quiet. The cuts and scratches on Violet's face had healed over. Diana had finished reading the first book to Violet and had started a new one. It was called *The Festival of Bells*. It took place in a Fairytale world. The story was about a gathering among friends to send the spirits of loved ones who had passed away into the next world. The story intrigued Diana. While Diana was reading, she would notice slight twitches from Violet. This gave her hope, and inspired her to continue reading.

In the story, everyone was given a bell and a metal rod when they were born. The two items had the owners name engraved into them. They were advised to keep the bell and rod safe and to decorate them as they pleased, however they wished to do so. When someone would pass away, their family would have them cremated and store their ashes in the bell, sealing the bottom so they could be kept together until the next festival. The festival would happen half way through the year and all of the families who had lost someone would gather. A funeral would be held for all of the deceased and then the ashes would be spread across a meadow and a final prayer said. The festival was not meant to be grim; they treated it like a party in honor of the departed. Once the ashes had been spread, a song would be played on the bells. At the end of the ceremony, the bells would be hung from a nearby tree for that year. Finally, a blessing was bestowed upon the tree every year by their leader.

Among the tents, there were groups of people. Many of them were holding bells with various drawings covering them. Violet noticed engravings on the bells with words she did not recognize. Diana led Violet into the crowd towards the Unicorn.

"Let me introduce you to him." Diana whispered to Violet before they were behind the Unicorn. "Greetings, Hestaphal!"

The majestic beast turned its head towards Diana, its body following in turn. "Hello again, Diana. It has been a long time since we last spoke."

Violet thought it looked awkward, the horse's lips forming Humanoid sounds. She was enchanted by its eyes however. The purple was soft yet hardened, as though the owner could be strict yet kind. And its fur looked incredibly soft from this close. Violet wanted so badly to pet it and treat it like a pony, but thought it would be better if she waited for now, at least until she knew him better.

"It has been long, Hestaphal. There appears to be many families this year." Diana's smile had waned with that.

"Indeed there is. The Manticore has become more active lately, killing for sport rather than just for sustenance." Hestaphal was looking at Violet. "I see you have brought a visitor. Who might she be?"

"Oh! My apologies. This is Violet Glendale, she came to the mother tree yesterday and I offered her a room. She came from the cherry forest." Diana put emphasis on the last words, leaning in as she said them.

"A Human?" The Unicorn's eyes had widened, he was clearly interested. "Is she the one who was attacked by Kenghala?"

"Who is... that?" Violet interrupted, she had never heard the name before and did not want to mess it up.

"The Manticore you met near the lake, his name is Kenghala. It's a wonder you survived; he rarely fails to catch his prey. Tell me; where are you from, girl? I have not seen one of your kind in a very long time."

"I'm not sure where it is relative to this place. I woke up on a lone hill where a tree called Tok-Nulon lives. I'm not sure how I got there."

A gong was hit among the tents and the crowd began to move into the meadow.

The Unicorn's head turned back. "I would like to talk to you after the festival, if you would be willing to."

"Of course." Violet so badly wanted to touch his fur when he was walking away.

"He seems to have taken an interest in you. I wonder what that could be...?" Diana was half talking to Violet, half talking to herself. "Oh well. Would you like to go and watch the festival?"

Violet was still thinking about the Unicorn's fur.

"Violet?"

"Hm? Oh! Sorry, I didn't hear you. Could you repeat that?"

"I asked if you would like to go and watch the festival."

"I would like to, yes." The Unicorn fur called to her.

"Are you okay?"

"Me? Yeah! I'm fine. Why?" Violet tried to hide her eyes. Too late.

"Because you seem kind of..." Diana grabbed Violet's shoulder and turned her to see her eyes. "...excited." Diana moved her hands to Violet's face, prying open eyelids and holding cheeks. "Did he put a spell on you, by chance?" Diana was thinking out loud once more. "You've certainly become better at hiding your thoughts." Diana let go of Violet's face. She had been holding tightly, leaving red marks on Violet's cheeks. "Come on, you might like to see the festival."

Violet followed hesitantly, she had found it very weird that Diana had acted that way. Had she actually hidden her thoughts? She hadn't put any effort into it.

Hestaphal was giving a speech. "Many of you have come this year. That is both reassuring and saddening. While we do this to honor our loved ones, we also must recognize the loss of them. I would like you all to share a few short words on behalf of your loved one."

A short speech was given by each member of the circle. They shared words of love, sadness and relief. They shared memories of their loved ones, and they wished them safe passage to the next life. Once the procession was complete, Hestaphal began once more.

"Uncover your bells, fellow mourners. Spread the ashes of the departed across the meadow upon which you stand, and say your final farewell." They all did just that, except for one. An Elf woman had clung to her bell longer than everyone else, tears running down her cheeks. The bell had been engraved with the name Mysro, it was the name of her husband. He had been a victim of Kenghala. They had found barely enough of his body to identify him, leaving his bell filled low with ashes. Eventually, the woman spread the ashes at her feet, unintentionally mixing them with her tears in the grass.

A prayer was said by Hestaphal, and the members of the circle all removed a metal rod from their bells, and together they played a song on them. The procession moved to a tree near the tents, each person hanging a bell on its very own branch. Finally, the Unicorn touched his horn to the tree. Its branches rattled gently, sending a chiming of bells outwards in all directions. A final cry rang out from the Phoenix overhead as it flew towards the mountains, its glow leaving the meadow in the shadow of the mother tree's canopy. The sun was peeking over the mountains, and with that, the festival was at an end.

Chapter Twelve

Daydreams

Daybreak came as the revelers began to dissipate. The rays of light snuck between the mountain tops, returning light to the meadow. Violet had already returned to her room but could not sleep due to the intruding sunlight. The tree was silent from root to canopy. The festival had drained everyone's energy, and today was recognized as a day of rest. Violet hadn't taken off her dress. She was sprawled out on the covers, her feet pointing to the window. The dress had gotten a bit dirty around the bottom trim, she had often forgot to lift it when she walked and left it to drag across the ground. Her eyes were open; she wasn't tired. Hours passed before Violet convinced herself to sleep and pass the time.

Violet dreamt of Kenghala. The beast was walking towards the body of a dying Elf, he was still trying to pull himself away. The Manticore lowered his head to the Elf, and opened his mouth. Blue ethereal looking dust traveled from all across the Elf's body into the beast's maw. The Elf writhed on the ground throughout the duration of the process, until the dust stopped, and so did the Elf.

Violet's dream changed at that moment. She was standing in front of the tree of bells, but something was wrong. The bells all had a hole melted through their sides. The wind rushing through the holes emitted a noise like a scream. It disturbed Violet. Ghosts appeared from the bells and had begun to reach towards her, whispering a name and making cries for help. She was tossing and turning on the bed when she was woken up by a sharp knocking sound.

Chapter Thirteen
Hestaphal's Arrangement

There came a knock at the door followed by a familiar voice, "Glendale, are you awake?" A handsome man that looked to be in his late twenties pulled the curtain aside to see into the room. His eyes were purple and his hair was grey. Not the grey of old age, however, but a lustrous grey, almost like silver. He wore a grey and white robe that reached down to his ankles. The robe was striped with vertical black lines and had golden buttons connecting the two sides down the center.

Violet awoke with a start, hitting her wrist on the bed frame. She was surprised to have company during this so called "day of rest", but she was glad to have company all the same. Violet sat up on her bed and turned her head to see the door. She saw the man, but did not recognize him. He walked into the room before she found words.

"I thought you said you would stay to talk after the festival?"

That was the voice! She hadn't placed it, but it was that of the Unicorn, Hestaphal. "Hestaphal? I thought you were a Unicorn?" Her wrist was starting to turn purple; she had hit it pretty hard.

"I was, yes. It is one of many forms I can take on. I am Hestaphal the shapeshifter. In short, I may turn into any creature that has a heart and the potential to move."

"I have a question for you."

"What is it?"

"Can you do magic?"

Hestaphal was bewildered. "I suppose, a magic of sorts, yes. Why do you ask?"

"Because Diana thought you put a spell on me."

"Oh, no, of course not. It's not that kind of magic; not enchantment. That is not what I would like to discuss, however. You are a human, yes?"

"Yeah. Why?"

Hestaphal ignored her question, "But you are not of this world, correct? I have served as a sort of symbolic leader for this realm for a very long time, and I have not seen your kind for centuries. They were defeated in a war by the mountain Trolls during the regime of Kairenax

Wilthren. None survived, so how is it that you are here?"

Violet only understood half of what the man had said to her. The combination of her lack of knowledge of this world and his rushed speaking made it very difficult for her to follow. "I don't know how I got here, honestly. I was walking through the street heading home when something hit me, and I woke up on a hill beside a tree called Tok-Nulon."

"Is it possible that you came from across the sea on the other side of the mountain range?"

"Well, I haven't been to Europe, but I am pretty sure they don't have Unicorns, Manticores, talking trees, or Phoenixes. So I'm going to go out on a limb here and say no, I didn't come from overseas."

"I didn't say anything about a 'U-rope', and there are these things that you speak of all across our world. Enough of that though, The Gazer has spoken to me of you, he told me that you do not belong here. However, even he is unsure of how you came to be in our world. He has spoken of your existence being a mistake." Hestaphal sat on the corner of the bed beside Violet. "I do not share his convictions, I believe you were brought here for a reason. Our world is coming to a breaking point, Glendale. The Trolls have allied with the Ogres and the Goblins, and have taken to calling themselves the Denizens of the Southern Marshes. The three tribes have never taken too kindly to the civilized races of the north, and they present a threat to us now. While they have not yet, we have reason to believe that they plan on waging war on the northern races; that would include the Elves, Dwarves, Fairies, Dryads and Capricorns, all of which you have met. There are many more races at stake whom you have yet to meet. The Denizens have many resources still to tap into. Kenghala is one of few Manticores to inhabit the northern regions, most of those beasts stay in the swamps. It is rumored that some Manticores have been seen with wings, soaring across the swamps. If this is true, then we may have greater problems yet. The Trolls can be a conniving group, I would wager that they are attempting to gain the favor of other clans in the south and to tame beasts for their use. The Cyclops' have always been a hermit tribe, keeping to themselves in their caves below the ground; they would be hesitant to join the war effort. The Minotaurs have long been envious of the northern races, they will be easily swayed by the Trolls to join the Denizens."

Violet was long lost. She recognized some of the names but new little about anything of this world's politics. "So what does this have to do with me?"

Hestaphal had been rambling when Violet interrupted him. "You are going to help us win this war to come."

Violet was looking at him through squinting eyes, "And how am I going to be able to help you with that?"

"The Gazer is annoyed by your presence, he wants nothing more than for you to be returned to where you belong. However, he has also rarely interfered with the affairs of our world. If we can promise him something that he wants, perhaps he will help us."

Violet stood up from the bed and crossed her arms, "You want to sacrifice me to someone? Do I have a say in this?" Violet was angry on the surface, but, underneath, she was scared for her life.

"Sacrifice? Of course not! We are a civilized people. The Gazer claims to have a way to return you to where you belong. If we have what he wants, which, you are what he wants, then we could gain his favor and possibly have him fight alongside us in the war."

Violet was momentarily relieved, and then excited. Latching onto Hestaphal's shoulders, Violet asks, "You said he could bring me home?"

"He claims to have a way, yes."

"Can I meet him?" Nothing mattered more to Violet than to have her family back, to see her friends again and to sleep in her own bed.

"Not yet, we need you as leverage to barter with him. If we brought you to him, he would send you back immediately and would have no incentive to help us. We will keep you safe and hidden from him until the war is over, then you can return."

Violet felt her heart quiver. How could he do this? Present her with a way home but deny her of it. Violet reeled back, and with all her force, slapped the shapeshifter across the face, leaving a red handprint on his skin. "I'm not something you can just use to barter with!"

Hestaphal put a hand to his face, the red on his face intensifying. "I understand that this may be difficult for you to approve of, but if you do this, many lives will be saved." He rose from the bed and crossed to the door. "Regardless, you have no choice in the matter; you will stay here at the mother tree for the duration of the war. You can make your stay enjoyable for yourself, or you can make it unpleasant, that is the choice you get."

Violet found herself alone once more. She now preferred to have no company. She finds her old close in the dresser, cleaned and mended. The stitching was very well done; Violet could not distinguish where the cut in her skirt had been from the rest of the fabric. She was angry with

Hestaphal now, how could he deny her the right to freedom? It was unjust. Taking her clothes with her, Violet decides to try and ease her mind with a bath.

Chapter Fourteen
Observation

The Beginning of Violet's captivity was not overly restraining; she was free to wander wherever she pleased, as long as she stayed within the tree line. However, that wouldn't be possible in the first place. A perimeter of guards had been established along the outskirts of the meadow, prohibiting her from leaving.

Violet hated Hestaphal now, and she resented Diana. She thought that Diana had planned this from the beginning, that she had been kind to Violet to convince her to stay long enough for Hestaphal to meet her.

Currently, Violet was laying on her bed. She missed her family more with each day. This was the third week she had spent in this world, her captivity had been going for nearly two weeks now, and it was quickly becoming miserable. There came a knock from the entrance.

"Violet, would you come with me? I have something that I would like to show you." It was Diana.

"Why? Are you going to lock me up now?" Violet hated not having the privacy of a door.

Diana frowned. "No, I have something that will make your time here more tolerable. It's at the base of the tree, so would you come and see?"

"Did you know he was going to do this?"

"Who was going to do what?"

"Hestaphal. Did you know he would imprison me?"

"I wouldn't call it imprisonment. You have the freedom to do whatever you would like as long as you stay within the trees."

"So you did know!"

"No, Violet, I didn't know. I hadn't spoken to Hestaphal in quite a long while, actually. I was surprised by his interest in you, but I didn't think he would go to this extent. The Gazer rarely condescends to talk to the 'lesser beings' of this world, as he says it. That he would talk to someone about you in the first place means that you truly are significant him."

"Which makes me all the more valuable." Violet pulled the blanket over her head.

"Darling, please come with me. I am trying to help you be entertained during your stay."

Violet so badly wanted something to do, she grew more and more bored with each passing day. Perhaps if Diana was telling the truth then it would be worth her time. It wasn't like Violet was doing anything right now anyways. "Fine."

"Wonderful! Follow me."

They proceeded down the stairs, meeting several others who averted their eyes from Violet. This made Violet uncomfortable, was something wrong with her appearance? Violet looked over the rail of the stairway towards the base, hoping to see just what Diana had talked about. There was nothing unusual about the scene, nothing that stood out to her. Arriving at the base of the tree, Violet still saw nothing. Diana brought her to a door behind a counter. She unlocked it with a small wooden key, and turned the handle, opening it with a creak. Behind the door were more stairs, but these were made of dirt after the third step, they were no longer in the tree. Jars of fireflies were placed in carved out sections of the stone walls, illuminating the otherwise pitch black stairwell.

After nearly a minute of stairs, the jars were no longer found in alcoves, but a blue light was now visible upon the walls. At the base of the stairs was a small and empty room. It was lit up with a blue light which emanated from a pool in the center of the room.

"What is this place?" Violet asked, keenly interested with the pool. It looked like a galaxy surrounded by a stone circle.

"This is the observatory. This pool grants the power of sight. You may say 'That's what eyes are for', but it is very different, so please, refrain from sarcasm. If you stare into the pool you will see our world. If you place your finger into the water of the map," Diana was demonstrating it as she explained, dipping her finger at a series of spots, "it will focus in on that area. You can continue to focus in until you can see the tiniest of insects or the ridges on a blade of grass." In the pool was an image of Capricorns playing in a lake. "If you would like to return to a more distant view, you have but to sweep both hands inwards through the pool." She followed her own instructions, and the pool returned to a picture of their world. "It goes different distances depending how much your hands move through it. Also, if you sweep with only one hand you can move across the landscape." She focused in on the Capricorns once more. One of them had pushed the other under the water and was fighting to keep them submerged. Diana turned to face Violet and leaned on the stone circle. "It shows you what is happening at that location in current time. You may have noticed also that you cannot hear anything from it, which is not a mistake, it has never conveyed sound. This is its greatest flaw. Though I believe you should be able to entertain yourself with it all the same." Diana stood up once more and walked over to Violet, setting her hands on Violet's shoulders. "I would ask that you do not speak of this to anyone, few others know of its location, and Hestaphal is not one of them. This place can act as your own haven, no one will bother you here." Diana took Violet's hand and placed the wooden key into it, closing Violet's hand around it. "This is the key to the door. Keep it with you at all times and give it to no one."

Violet was excited to have something to do, but she was caught up on the name. "The only observatories I've seen had telescopes looking at the stars."

"I know not of what you speak, I have never heard of something called a 'tellaskope'. The observatory is made possible through magic. It would be the only logical explanation."

Violet said nothing.

"Anyways, would you like to give it a try? The possibilities are endless and every day brings new sights."

"Okay. So, that's all it takes? Dabbing your finger?"

"Yes, it's simple really."

Violet walked over to the edge of the stone circle and leaned over the water's edge. The pool still showed the lake with the Capricorns, they were now just floating in the water. Violet swept her hands through the pool. It reminded her of using her phone, except it was much larger than her phone, and she used both hands instead of two thumbs. The map presented itself once more. Violet did not recognize anything at first, but after analyzing it for a few moments she saw the lone hill with Tok-Nulon, and near it, the lake she had swam in. She took notice of the mountain range, how it split the continent in two. Violet sets her finger onto the center of the hill, and the map becomes more detailed. She repeats this until she can see the tree in detail. There is nothing else to see on the hill, nothing out of the ordinary. Diana had come closer and was now watching over Violet's shoulder.

Returning to the map, she decides her next destination. She sees a cluster of mountains to the south, they stand apart from the mountain range. She focuses in on them and finds a one-eyed creature standing facing a group of burly Humanoids. The one eyed creature held a tree trunk in his left hand and had a horn protruding from his forehead above his lone eye. His skin was a yellowing beige, akin to that of old parchment. The other creatures had a variety of shapes and skin colors but all had large noses. There were eight total, three of which had brown skin, nearly the shade of dry dirt. Two of the others had green skin, similar to that of a rotting pear. Two others had skin that looked like the desert sand. The last one stood out the most to Violet. Its skin was as black as charcoal. The rest of its appearance was much different than the rest of its group as well. It stood over a foot taller than the rest of them, its body was muscular, unlike the others whose limbs were bulky with fat. The two characteristics that stood out most above all others were its eyes, that were a bright red, burning like fire on coal, and that it had tusks that jutted out from the sides of its mouth, they curled at the ends, pointing to the sky. None of the others had tusks.

Diana took a sharp breath close to Violet's ear.

"What is it?" Violet asked.

"Those are Trolls. If they are talking to the Cyclopes, then they must be nearly prepared for war."

"How can you tell that their almost ready just from them talking to a Cyclops?"

"The other races would need time to prepare. The Cyclopes would be the very last ones they would approach. A Cyclops does not prepare for anything; when they go to war they do not bring swords or flails, they tear out the nearest tree for their weapon. The other races all take the time to make something to fight with at least. I must go inform Hestaphal that the war approaches. It is a fortunate happening that you would find this on your first search."

With that, Violet was alone once more. There was a mix of emotions for her. She was excited for the war, because it meant she could leave and go home sooner, but at the same time she was afraid and worried. What if the war dragged on for a very long time? Or what if the Denizens were to win the war? Would she ever get home? There was nothing that she could do to change the outcome. She was helpless.

Chapter Fifteen
Call to Arms

A meeting had been called, any available emissaries from the northern races were to be present at the mother tree before sundown. Hestaphal now stood in front of the gathering. Few people among them knew of the reason for this meeting. The gathering was held in the courtyard of the great tree, so that the aquatic races could be present.

If Diana was to be believed, then they were entering difficult times. Hestaphal recognized most of the emissaries from past reunions. He was glad that so many people could meet on such short notice. There were representatives from nearly every race. The Elf king had sent his personal advisor with his own bodyguard. The Dwarves had sent a party of three. The races of the water folk had all sent one representative from their kingdom: a Mermaid, a Capricorn and a water sprite. The Gnome people had sent two of their greatest minds. A flock of Fairies were sitting among the branches. Several Dryads had collected, and a single Centaur was sent by their chief.

"Gather around everyone, we have much to discuss." Hestaphal had commenced the meeting.

The group of fifteen formed a circle, implementing one of the larger pools into their circle for the water folk to participate.

"Some of you know why we are here, others do not. So that everyone is on the same page, the Trolls have formed a clan called The Denizens of the Southern Marshes. This clan is more than just the Trolls however, with them there are Ogres, Goblins, Minotaurs and Cyclopes that we know of. There could easily be more that we do not know of. We are here today to discuss an alliance, to create a unified kingdom for the greater good of all of our people. We do not know how much time we have until they invade, it could be a day, or it could be two months. We should be prepared for them at any time. Before we begin, we should have a formal introduction and we should present our concerns to everyone. I will start. My name is Hestaphal, I am a shapeshifter who speaks for the wilds and the guild of transformation. We are afraid of the possibility that the southern races will be invading sooner than later, and we need to know that the northern races will be prepared to stand by us in war."

The first to step forward was the Centaur. He stood nearly eight feet tall and his front and rear legs stood six feet apart from each other. His hair war red and was not quite shoulder length. He wore a brown leather chest plate that was studded with a quiver strung across his waist and a bow on his back, held in place by a belt. "My name is Creindal, I represent the Centaur tribe of the eastern plains. My chief knew of the reason for this meeting, and I bear his concerns, along with the rest of our tribe. We do not want our plains to be scarred with the blood and destruction of war and ridden with corpses. We wish to fight the Denizens to the south in the dividing forest."

Next was the Mermaid, raising her hand to be noticed. Her hair was a fair shade of blue, and her eyes were green. Her scales created a visual illusion, there was a blue line of scales followed by a purple, then a pink, then a line of purple once more, then a blue. However, as her tail moved, the colored lines rearranged themselves. She wore next to nothing, having only a small covering made of seaweed over her bosom. "My Queen has sent me to bear witness to this congregation. My name is Miulein. My Queens concerns are that of her people. While the southern races cannot directly harm us, they have the potential to pollute our waters with their crude blacksmithing and forging, and for this reason we will fight alongside your forces if you battle near water. My people, like the Capricorns, can travel between any bodies of water in our world, so we will be prepared as long as the fight is close enough to the shore."

The two Gnomes stepped forward. They stood at three feet tall. One of them had brown hair and a brown beard, and the other's hair and beard were grey. They both wore spectacles over their eyes. The grey haired man spoke first, "My name is Baird, and this is my son, Guile. Our colony has sent us to share our views. The Gnomes have never been a people for fighting, however, we see the threat that this war brings. While we will not fight alongside you, we will supply you with whatever arms or technology that we can." They stepped back into the circle.

The Capricorn was next, she could barely contain herself. She waved her hand quickly back and forth to get everyone's attention. She wore no clothing, she had no need to. Her bottom half was covered with scales, and her top half was concealed with fur that rose up from where her hips would be and connected below her chest and ended at her collar bone, leaving her stomach and neck exposed. Her purple hair fell in curls around her horns. "My name is Leira. I was chosen by Pricus, the father of the Capricorns. His will is what's best suited for the Capricorn people, so we follow his beliefs and concerns. Pricus wanted me to inform you all that we will help from the water when we can. Most of us can manipulate the water with magic, so we can help from a distance."

The Elf advisor stepped forward, his bodyguard in tow. He had amber eyes on white skin. He stood just short of six feet tall, and his long light green hair reached the cuffs of his white robe "My name is Sikator, I am the chief advisor for his majesty, the king of Elves. The Elves are reluctant to fight, but our people will do what we must to defend our beloved forests. We are at your side."

One of the Dryads stepped forward. She stood taller than the Elf, but shorter than the Centaur. Her brown hair was littered with leaves and it reached to the back of her knees. "My name is Daisy. My sisters and I speak for the trees. For the preservation of our world; the trees and the earth nymphs will join you in this war."

The water sprite flew out of the pool over to the Fairies. They discussed amongst themselves for a short time, and then flew over to the Dryad. The water sprite whispered into Daisy's ear, and she conveyed their message. "The Fairies have potent magic as well, and are willing to help with enchanting and ranged attacks, but refuse to fight in close quarters." The water sprite was nodding the whole time. After Daisy had finished, she flew back into the pool and the Fairies returned to their branch.

The Dwarves stepped forward. The Dwarves were portly men that stood a little over four feet tall. They each had their own beard that was braided into different patterns. All three of them had red hair. The center Dwarf was designated as speaker. "My name is Aldreit, to my right is Gein, and to my left is Breitol. The Dwarves will aid in this war, but our people reserve the right to retreat if we believe it to be the best course of action."

Hestaphal stepped forward once more. "Now that everyone has shared their concerns, and we are all familiar with each other, let us discuss logistics."

The group discussed strategy and army organization. Each party brought forward different possibilities and tactics. They ran inventory of their resources and their armories and gave a rough estimation of the number of soldiers each could provide for the cause. After nearly eight hours of deliberation, they had come up with a finalized plan that they would put to use.

"Let us go over it one more time, to bring it back to our leaders with a clear memory." Hestaphal had changed into a Unicorn once more and was laying in the grass. The others had taken a seat in it as well, except the water folk, who leaned on the edge of the pools' stone wall. "We will battle on the coast of the Lake of Lenidral, where the Sea Folk and the Capricorns can aid us. Our front lines will be composed of the shapeshifters from the Guild of Transformation and the Centaurs. Dwarves will take up the middle of our force, backed by the Elves who will be our archers. Gnomes, you agreed that you can operate war machines in the back lines, yes?"

"Indeed. We will build them for the war and we can operate them for you as well."

"Splendid. Dryads, you and the trees will hold the dividing forest, aided by the Fairies magic. This will force the enemy towards the Lake. The Phoenix has already agreed to help us as well. We will not need to worry about aerial attacks, so we can focus all of our efforts on one area. Our odds are looking very good."

"Wait. How is it that we will not need to worry about enemy aerial forces? The Phoenix is mighty, but he may not be enough to hold back the entire enemy aerial assault." The Centaur asked, he doubted Hestaphal's plan.

"If all goes as planned, The Gazer will be our ally in the war to come. He will be more than enough to deal with any threats the enemy can produce from the sky as well as on land."

"The Gazer? Why would he be willing to help us?" The members of the congregation were wide-eyed.

"Because, we have something that he wants very dearly. Have you all heard of the Human who appeared on the lone hill?" The entire congregation nodded their understanding. "The Gazer wants nothing more than to send her back to where she came. No one knows how the Human came to be here, except for The Gazer. The Human is in our possession, and we will use her to force The Gazer into action."

"And if he does not help us? How will we cope with such a blow?"

"If he refuses, then the Shapeshifters will do what we can to aid the Phoenix."

They were relieved to hear there was a contingency plan, but were still worried. The representatives said their farewells, and left for their kingdoms. A heavy weight was on each of their shoulders. If the plan was rejected by any of their leaders, they could not guarantee the time to create a new one. The war may soon be upon them.

Chapter Sixteen
A Guilty Conscience

Once the other envoys had left, Hestaphal was alone. He did not leave, because he felt an obligation. He felt that he must apologize to Violet once more before he left. He looked up at the tree from the courtyard, at Violet's window, and saw her watching from it. She must have seen him look at her, because she closed the window immediately.

He began his ascent of the stairwell, lost in thought. He didn't like the idea of imprisoning a girl, even if it was for the greater good. She would hate him for having done it, if she did not already, that is. She would probably ignore him when he came to console her, perhaps even strike him once more. But if it eased his mind, even a little, then it was worth the time.

When he focused again on the steps, he was long past her doorway, nearing the top of the tree. He waited to descend, deciding whether to go straight there or to continue upwards. He was reluctant to face her, but he knew it had to be done. Eventually, he continued on up the stairs instead. He stops at the final doorway from the top of the tree and knocks on the wall beside it.

"Come in." A voice answered, a cold tone lining its authority.

He enters into Diana's room. The furnishings were all various shades of green and pink. He sees her sitting on a stool in front of her mirror, grooming her hair.

"What is it Hestaphal?" She asked without turning away from the mirror. There was irritation in her voice.

"I wanted to ask your permission before I see the girl."

"And why did you think you would need my permission? You're an adult, aren't you?"

The condescension in her voice irked him. "You know very well that it pains me just as much as you to have to keep her here."

She sat up from the stool and faced him. "You don't *have* to do anything, Hestaphal. It is your own choice to take away her freedom."

"If the northern races are to survive, then we must keep her here. It is the only way for The Gazer to help us."

"And who says we need The Gazer for victory? Do you doubt the resolve of the northern races?"

"The northern races doubt their own resolve. They do not wish to fight this war; no one does. But we cannot sit idly by as the Denizens come into our lands and slaughter our people, we must fight back."

"Have you thought of how the girl must feel? Being held against her will?"

"Of course I have! Every day that we must keep her longer is another day that I wish had never happened."

"Then why not end those days and bring her to The Gazer?"

"Because if we give him the girl then he will not help us."

"You do not know that."

"He does not believe a debt need be repaid. This is the only way to gain his aid."

Diana sat down at the stool once more. "Why did you come to me in the first place?"

"To have your permission to speak to her."

"No, you came to me first for a reason not to speak to her. You do not want to face her, because you are ashamed. I will not deny you from speaking to her, so you may go now and talk to her. Besides, I do not decide who may or may not speak to her; she decides that for herself."

Hestaphal would not admit it to himself, but she was right. Why did she always have to be right...?

He exits through doorway and starts down the stairs once more.

Once he was at Violet's door, he paused. He was psyching himself up. Deeming himself prepared, he raises his hand, and raps the wood three times. No one answers. Perhaps she is ignoring him. He knocks once more. Nothing. Pulling the curtain aside so that he can see the room, he sees no one. He moves to the center of the room. From the washroom he hears water, not running water, but water being splashed. She must be in the bath. Staying out of view from the doorway, he knocks on its wall. The sound of water being displaced rapidly is heard, but she does not answer.

"Glendale, it's Hestaphal. I would like to talk with you."

She does not answer.

"I know you can hear me. I would like to apologize to you for keeping you here."

She does not answer.

"I will wait for you." Moving from the door to the bed, he sits to wait. Two hours pass. She does not come into the room. He gets up and knocks at the door once more.

She does not answer.

"Would you grant me your audience?"

Again, she does not answer.

Hestaphal knew how to stop her game. "Oh, I understand, would you like me to come to you? If it's too mu-"

Water was heard spilling over onto the floor. "No! Don't you dare come in here!"

"Then I would ask that you come out here."

"Did it occur to you that I don't want to talk to you?"

"Yes, innumerable times. All the same, I would ask you to please come and speak with me."

He heard a sigh. Followed by more water. "Don't you dare look."

"It never crossed my mind."

When she finally entered the room, she was wearing the blue and white dress from the festival night and her hair was still wet. She sat in the doorway with crossed arms and just stared at Hestaphal, waiting.

"Thank you for your willingness to speak with me. I would just like to say that I am sorry for keeping you here, even if such an apology is insubstantial for the time that you will lose while here. I would ask that you take a minute to see things from my perspective." He stood up from the bed and walked into the center of the room once more. "My world is at stake. The Denizens will be relentless once they invade, nothing but death will stop them. You offer us that solution."

"It sounds more like you're calling me a murderer by saying that."

"That is not my intention at all; a poor choice of words, perhaps. On the contrary, you are a savior. What I mean to say is that without you, we would all perish. Because you are here, we have the means to barter with The Gazer. While I know that you will never have this time back, I hope that you can take heart in the fact that you spent this time saving thousands of lives."

Violet walked over to the window, opening it and leaning on its sill, staring out over the forest. A long silence passed between them, until finally Violet answered. "It's hypocritical of me to say this, but that sounded more like an excuse than an apology."

"But will you accept it?"

"If it gets you to leave me alone, then yes. I accept your apology."

"It is rather rude of you to dismiss me like that. I have come to you with a sincere apology, and you accept it solely to be rid of me."

Violet turns to face him, arms crossed once more. "Oh, I'm rude? You are the one who's keeping me against my will in a world where I don't belong. You come to me asking for forgiveness to ease your own mind for a crime that you committed while I stay trapped here. I would say that's pretty rude, Unicorn boy."

"So, we are both hypocrites." He turns and walks towards the door. "Farewell Violet, for both of our sakes, I pray this will be a short war." And with that, he left.

Chapter Seventeen

The Denizens

Two weeks later, a meeting had been called by the Troll Chieftain; anyone who was joining the war was to be present. The Chieftain had charcoal skin and tusks; this is what set him apart from the other Trolls. The other Denizens called him Trygon.

Currently he stood in front of his fellow Denizens, he was giving a final speech to raise their moral and to fuel their hatred. He wore a set of black chain armor, darker than his own skin, and carried a double headed axe, which had a black and red jewel in the hilt, in his right hand.

"For centuries the northern races have frowned upon us, they exiled our ancestors to these swamps and deserts and had all but forgotten us! Today! Today is the beginning of our return! We will crush their pathetic lives and grind their bones to dust! We will burn their mother tree and tear down their mountains! We will reclaim what is ours! Let the war begin!"

A cheer arose from the entire army. "March!" The army began their journey to the north. It would take three days of travel before they arrived.

Chapter Eighteen
The Gazer

Hestaphal had spoken to The Gazer at his temple. His temple was in a remote location in the mountains, near the tallest peak. Its walls were illuminated by The Gazer's body. The negotiations could have gone better; The Gazer was outraged with Hestaphal's impudence.

"You would deny me the girl?" Cold hatred lined the words with an icy tone. "You ask for my assistance in a war, because you have little faith in your own people. That is not the trait of a leader, illusionist. Give me the girl and perhaps I will aid you in your petty affairs." His words were like icicles, spearing into the mind and leaving cold.

"That will never happen Gazer. I know as well as you do that you would have no intention of aiding my people if I gave you the girl. You will help us in battle, and then you can have the girl once the war is won."

The light on the walls flashed red and settled into orange. "And what if I killed you now and took the girl? There are only so many places you could hide her, it would not take long to find her."

"Then you would be condemning thousands to their deaths. You would be relinquishing all honor that you have in exchange for a girl."

The lights on the wall flushed red and his voice changed, it was now a fire burning through a forest of nerves, searing the mind. "Your honor means nothing, it is a petty illusion that holds no value in reality. Honor will bring you nothing substantial, and it will not save your life. That girl is a disturbance in our world, she should not stay for this long! If you would not bring me the girl it would be a declaration of rebellion against your world in a whole, not an act of defiance towards me."

"Gazer, you are the warden of our world, I would ask that you fulfill your charge and keep peace between two warring nations."

The light on the wall changed to blue, and the room got colder.

"Every world has wars, it is the nature of sentience. You challenge another group of beings to prove your superiority only to either be defeated or to be victorious. You mortals play with life and death like it is a game, yet you frown upon the wars that are of your own making. This war has been six centuries in the making, yet your people were too foolish to prevent it. You speak of me condemning thousands to death, yet your ancestors were the ones who condemned you to death. They tore a rift between the northern and the southern races. The titles of northern and southern are proof. If you truly did not want this war to happen, you would have found a way to end your conflicts with the Denizens through diplomacy, rather than leave them in their despair of defeat for them to plot their revenge. This war is the repercussion of half a millennium of resentment, and its foundation is hatred."

A long silence passed between them, the light on the walls changed to green. "If you would like my help, two conditions must be fulfilled."

"My people and I are prepared to do anything for your assistance."

"The first condition is this: You will bring the girl to me after this war, no matter the outcome. The second: You will not make the same mistakes as your ancestors, you will gather the northern races after your victory and forgive the southern races for their current and past transgressions, as well as apologize for your own offenses, and you will strive to bring long lasting peace between your two nations. You will not condemn them to the swamps or the deserts, but welcome them into the plains and forests of the north. If you fail to meet the first condition, I will take your life without remorse, and the girl will be sent home all the same. The second, however, if you fail to meet this condition, I will do nothing. The consequence of not meeting the second condition is for history to repeat, and this war will happen once more in centuries to come. I will not be as forgiving when your descendants come to ask for my aid in their own war, I will tell them of this conversation, and deny them."

A weight was lifted from Hestaphal's shoulders. "If this is what it takes, then we will make peace between our two lands, no matter the cost. The girl will be brought to you in the week following the end of the war."

"Go now, shapeshifter, your people need you. I will be there when I am needed most in the battles to come."

Hestaphal dropped to one knee. "Thank you, Gazer."

"Do not thank me, I am not doing this for you, I am doing this for the future of this world. Now go."

Hestaphal left the temple, flying away as a raven.

Inside the temple, the walls had turned purple.

Chapter Nineteen
The Messengers Return

Creindal entered the stone circle of the Centaur shamans. His tribe had been waiting since his departure the day before for him to return. The stone circle was ringed with the members of his tribe. The chieftain was waiting at the far end of the stone circle, kneeling in the grass. Creindal approached his chief, and bowed before him.

"Sit," The chief said, "Tell us of your journey. What information have you brought to us?" The Chief had gray hair that reached below his wrinkled chin, and his body had scars in various spots across its entirety. He was the oldest in the tribe, and was appointed chief due to his knowledge and wisdom of their world.

Creindal sat in the grass. "Plans have been made, and I believe it would be wise to accept them. We will be fighting near the Lake of Lenidral. The Centaurs and the Shapeshifters will form the front ranks, followed by the Dwarves and then the Elves as archers. The army fights near the lake so that the Sea Folk may aid us. War machines will be operated by the Gnomes at the back of the army."

"But what of the air?"

"The Phoenix has agreed to aid us, and Hestaphal claims to have a way of convincing The Gazer to aid us."

Whispers ran among the crowd of onlookers. "The Gazer? Why would he be willing to help us? What could possibly convince that old guard to take action?"

The chief was visibly doubtful.

Creindal continued. "Hestaphal has the Human girl in his possession. It appears that The Gazer would love nothing more than to have her."

The chief was thinking. "I see. Perhaps he is not as much of a mad man as I had thought. Very well. The Centaurs will follow this plan to their last breath; it shall be done."

War was coming, and the Centaurs would fight it.

***

The trio of Dwarves returned home to the mountain of their

people. The streets of their cave city were alive with pedestrians. The trio had a tough time navigating through the dense population. No one from the mountain except for the king and his advisor knew that they had left, let alone why they had gone. But the Dwarves were a loyal people, they would follow their king to hell and back.

Aldreit walked in front, followed by Breitol and then Gein. Pushing through the crowds, they eventually reached the colossal iron door of the king's chamber. Hammering the door with his fist, Aldreit waited to be let in. A loud clang was heard from behind the door, followed by the sound of metal on stone.

The door opened into a large room filled with gold coins and jewels surrounding a throne. Tapestries were hung from the walls depicting wars long past. The king had a black beard and was wearing a red robe that was flecked with gold. His gold crown was studded with gemstones.

"Brave trio, come forward." He paused to cough, "Tell me what you have heard." The king was sick, his health had been declining for the last month.

The trio moved forward, kneeling in front of the throne. "My liege," Aldreit started, "The war is imminent. The other races would like our help for it. They have placed us in the center of the army."

The king took a second to catch his breath. "Then in the center you shall be. Spread the word, the Dwarves will fight! Tell everyone to gather their supplies. We will send a courier tomorrow morning to share the news, and we will arrive by the end of the week."

"My liege, you do not intend to join us, do you?"

"A king should fight alongside his people until his last breath, I would have it no other way. Aldreit, should I pass away during this war, you, being my eldest, shall take up the throne."

***

The giddy Capricorn, Leira, approached Pricus. She was in his lake not even an hour after the assembly had disbanded. She was now bubbling over with excitement.

"Pricus! Pricus!" She shouted as she approached him. "I've brought news about the war! Just like you said to, Pricus!"

"Good, little one! Please, do share it with me." Pricus looked slightly different than the other Capricorns. He was a man with the lower half of a fish and the horns and fur of a goat, all his fur and hair was brown, except three things distinguished him from the rest: his horns were much larger than the other Capricorns, he had more fur across his body, and he was much larger in comparison to the other Capricorns.

"Well, Pricus, they started out talking about where they were from and what their concerns were, I shared fourth and then after that it was really boring listening to them. But I stuck it out and got the information you asked for!"

"Perfect, Leira! Please, do tell me what you heard."

"The northern races are going to war with the southern races near the Lake of Lenidral. They want it to be at the lake so we can help them, along with the Sea Folk. Is war going to be fun, Pricus?"

"War is never fun, Leira. Please, dear, if you would; could you show me how your aquamancy is coming along?"

"Sure, Pricus! What would you like to see?"

"How about you start with an aqua lance. Just throw one into the air."

"Okay!" Leira did just that, she held her hands above the lake and pulled a lance of water from it. She threw it into the air, and it exploded into tiny water droplets once it was high above the lake.

"Very good, Leira! Keep practicing your other techniques too. I'm sorry to shoo you away, but I have to make preparations. Could you do me a huge favor, Leira?

"Sure!"

"Okay, I would like you to gather as many of your brothers and sisters as you can, tell them all to keep practicing their aquamancy as well, and tell them to come to my lake in a few days."

"Sure thing, Pricus! See you later!"

"Farewell, Leira!"

And with that she left to find her siblings.

***

Baird and his son returned to the Gnome colony with what they believed to be good news; the Gnomes did not have to fight up close, they had only to build and operate their own machines. They went to the Mayor's office in town center to discuss with him.

"My son and I both think that we have a good deal here. We aren't in any danger, far at the back of the fight; no enemies will be coming from the forest and the sky will be covered. We only have to do what we're used to."

The mayor was wearing a miniature tuxedo with a top hat and monocle. His pipe had a steady stream of smoke coming from it. "It would be foolish to decline such an offer. It is, as you say, a good deal. Send word to Heidskun, the Gnomes will follow through, and put up signs to inform the engineers: Urgent Work Order – Catapults, Ballistae and Trebuchets. All able engineers are to change their current projects to these three things. Go now, spread the word!"

The father and son duo left for the paper factory immediately, they would need many posters.

***

Sikator approached his king, bodyguard in tow. The Elf king was in a meeting with his generals.

"Ah! Sikator, come forward. What news have you brought me? All good news, I would hope." The King was as slender as his people, with silver hair running past his shoulders and a crown of silver upon his head.

"I would like to think so, your Majesty. The Shapeshifter, Hestaphal, has forged a plan for war with the help of envoys from each of the northern races. The Elves are to be archers in the rear ranks of the army."

"I see," The King picked up his bow with an arrow on the strings. Throwing an apple up and away from him, he fires the bow, splitting it in two. A clean cut down the center. "We should be more than capable to hold our own then." He says with a chuckle as the apple hits the floor.

"Yes, I believe we shall. Your Majesty, how would you like the news to be spread of the war?"

"That, Sikator, is why my generals are here. We plan on making an announcement tonight. The Elves will fight."

***

Miulein sat inside the Queen's antechamber waiting to be welcomed into her presence. She was admiring the architecture of the palace, and the stonework of the floor. Each stone had been colored, and they came together to make a picture of the city as seen from above. Miulein admired the white marble pillars of the antechamber, and the glass ceiling that opened a view to the ocean life above.

The door to the Queen's chamber opened, and the Queen's servant came from it. "You have been invited in, Envoy."

Miulein entered into the Queen's chamber. Its walls went up for nearly thirty meters, riddled with inscriptions of the ancient language of the Sea Folk and with carvings of historic occasions. The room had stained glass windows that colored the room in its entirety.

"My dear Daughter! You have returned! Please, do come closer." Miulein swam across the throne room. The Queen was laying on a large stone seat, her tail hanging over one arm and her pink hair hanging over the other. Miulein was used to her mother staying seated, even when she was greatly excited, royal composure and what not. "So? Can we help in the war? I dread to think what would happen if we could not aid the land walkers."

"Yes, Mother, we will be able to help them. They plan to fight near the Lake of Lenidral. Our purpose is for ranged magic artillery. However, I believe they would appreciate our restorative magic as well."

"Smart girl!" The Queen snapped her fingers and winked at Miulein. "So, when do they plan to convene at the lake?"

"In a few days they will be gathering. The Shapeshifter said something quite incredible." Miulein said looking through the ceiling. "He said that he plans to have The Gazer as our ally in the battles to come."

"Oh?" The Queen was interested, her eyes had widened. "And did he say how he plans to do that? The Gazer has always been neutral, never preferring one to another. I find it difficult to believe millennia of sameness could be broken with ease."

"He claims to have what The Gazer wants most. A human who came to be in our world."

"A human? Preposterous, they have been dead for centuries, there is not even the slightest possibility of one being in our world."

"I thought so too, but I saw her in one of the windows of the mother tree when I was at Heidskun."

The Queen's eyes narrowed. "A living Human... How could that possibly be?"

The Queen dismissed Miulein to spread the word among the Sea Folk, they would aid the Land Dwellers.

***

A meeting was being held at the lake shore. All of the Fairies, from the sea, from the sky, and from the land, were to meet.

All sorts of Fairies came to the meeting. The hermit Fairies of the caves, with their purple translucent wings and luminescent hair; the cloud Fairies, with their white skin and foggy eyes; the fire Fairies, with their gowns of living flame; the water Fairies, with their liquid limbs; and the forest Fairies, with their grassy gowns and various insect wings. Even among the individual types of Fairies, there was much variety, the color of their hair for instance, or the exact shade of their skin.

A rainbow winged forest Fairy called order to the gathering. "Everyone! We need to focus, there will be time for talking later! The other races are going to war, and they would like our help. All we would have to do is give magic support from hiding. They would like some of us to hide among the trees and hurl magic, but each of you could work in your own element. If we don't help them now, we will probably have to put up with much worse neighbors, like Ogres or Trolls. They aren't even pleasant to look at."

A response of agreeance ran through the crowd.

A fire Fairy raised her hand. "So, it's pretty much going to be like our games, except actually harmful? That sounds easy."

"It will be easy, it's exactly like the games we play, but we're playing for keeps this time, so we have to be more serious."

One by one the different groups of Fairies eventually all agreed; they wanted to throw some real magic, not the kind that just broke into dust on contact.

* * *

Hestaphal's day was not yet over; He had apologized to Violet, he had spoken with The Gazer, but he still had to bring his information to the Guild.

The Gazer's shrine was a long distance from the Guild, but Hestaphal was approaching quickly; his day would soon be over. The head of the Guild had informed Hestaphal he would leave his window open with a candle on the sill. The Guild was located in the hills near a lone mountain opposite the mountain range. It was built among the trees of the forest, easily missed by the untrained eye. The mountain it was built against was a very special one, for on the side of the Guild, coniferous trees grew, but against its other face, there were cherry blossoms.

Hestaphal spotted the tiny flame in the night, and began his descent. The Guild resembled a very large log cabin. It appeared that way on the inside as well, the only thing that made it special was what happened inside its walls; the practice of Shapeshifting. As the trees drew closer, the darkness abated. As an initiation into the Guild of Transformation, every new member was blessed with an enchantment, the same one was bestowed upon each member. This enchantment affected the Shapeshifter's eyes, granting them clear vision when they came within a certain vicinity of the Guild, giving sight as clear as day no matter the weather nor the time.

Hestaphal landed on the floor of the room and returned to his Humanoid form. Standing up, Hestaphal was greeted with a book to the back of his head.

"Ye almost knocked the candle over when ye flew in, ye bird brain." The head of the Guild was a Dwarf with a heavy Irish accent, though it wasn't considered Irish in this world. "Be more careful next time."

"Yes, Archibald." Hestaphal said, rubbing the back of his head.

Archibald began once more, "So? What did they think of that mighty fine plan o' mine?"

"They were all doubtful, as was I when you first told me, but they came through when I told them of my new findings. A card has found its way into our hand, Archibald, and it may just make up the difference we needed for this war."

"And what might that be, feather boy?" He asked while taking a raven plume from Hestaphal's hair.

"The Human girl that arrived."

Archibald sat back into his rocking chair, stretching his legs out. "Ye don't say? And I assume ye want me to believe that The Gazer himself gave you the girl before flying off into the sunset under a double rainbow." He finished his sarcastic comment and picked up his mug of tea, taking a large mouthful and downing it. "How's a girl going to help win a war, genius?"

"Actually, it didn't happen that way. She found her way to Heidskun. She will be a great help because The Gazer wants the girl, and I am prepared to give her to him, on one condition, that he accepted."

"And what might that be, lad." He took another gulp of tea.

"To help us win the war."

Archibald lurched forward, spraying tea from between tight lips across his bed covers. "Damnit all! What's that ye say? That old wretch is actually gonna do something for once?" He sat up and began stripping the bed of its covers. "I'll believe it when I see it. All he ever does is watch anyways, physical exercise is a wee bit much for him."

"Have you ever met The Gazer, Archibald?"

"I haven't had to, why do ye ask?"

"You might be surprised then when you see him."

***

The Dryads had lied at the meeting; the trees had not yet agreed to help yet, but they had no other option. They would be convinced.

The trees were bullheaded; they did not like getting involved with matters that weren't their own. If it meant possible danger to them, they preferred to stay out of it.

This was the Dryad's job, to get the trees into action. They had started communing with the trees not even an hour after the meeting at Heidskun had ended, and were still trying to convince the trees days later.

"The Denizens will cut our roots if we act against them." An elder tree stated.

"Perhaps, but they will burn you down if they succeed in their war." Daisy rebuked. "What do you all love most in this world?"

"The mother tree of Heidskun." Several dozen voices answered in unison.

"The Denizens will burn it to the ground without second thought. If you want to save the mother tree, you must not allow the Denizens to pass through your woods."

The same arguments were brought up time and time again, and the same answers were given each time. It took four full days for Daisy to finally convince them.

"Dear Dryads, the trees understand that you would only argue with us if it was for the greater good of the forests. It is for this reason that we will concede; we will aid in the war as you advise us."

A collective sigh of relief came from all of the Dryads; their duty was done.

Chapter Twenty

Slow Days

Violet spent most of her days in the Observatory, often times just looking at the cherry blossom forest. She found that looking at the trees eased her mind, made her relax a bit. Diana would come down into the Observatory from time to time to talk with Violet. This was one of those times.

"Violet, someone wants to talk to you. They went to your room to look for you but they couldn't find you there. I told them I knew where you were and to wait upstairs. You best not keep them waiting."

"Who is it?" Violet asked. She did not want to talk with Hestaphal. "If it's Hestaphal tell him to leave."

"It isn't. I think you might want to talk to him." And Diana went back up the stairs.

Him? Who could that be? Violet couldn't think of anyone who would want to talk to her, everyone had been avoiding eye contact with her for over a week, and now someone wanted to talk? It might be worthwhile.

Violet found that the stairs seemed shorter than usual. She was excited to see who it could be, as long as it wasn't Hestaphal, or that disgusting Dwarf, then she would be happy, she thought to herself.

The door was already open at the top of the stairs, lighting up the last few steps with the sparse shreds of sunlight that could reach it. Diana was standing beside the doorway, waiting for Violet.

"He's waiting in that room," she said, pointing at a door across the lobby, "And get that frown off of your face; you look like you're ready to murder someone."

"What? I wasn't trying to look upset." Violet now felt self-conscious about her face. "Is this better?" She asked, casting a worried smile at Diana.

"Not by much, dear. Don't worry! Just be normal, okay? Don't look like you want to kill someone, and don't look like someone's trying to kill you, that's all." She clapped Violet on the back and sent her on her way.

Was her smile really that bad? Diana had Violet worried now. How could she talk to someone calmly now that she was so caught up in her appearance? This was another thing very similar to Violet's mother; she could really make you worry at the worst time.

Violet stopped in front of the door. Did she knock? Did she just walk in? Violet sat there for a few seconds before turning to Diana. Diana gestured for her to enter the room with a forward sweeping motion with her left hand. Violet responded with knocking her fist on an imaginary wall, and a shrug. Diana shook her head and faked opening a door. Violet ended up knocking anyways. An Elfin eared boy with blond hair answered the door.

Violet took a sharp breath. "You!" She could already feel her face reddening, that moment still lingered in her memory.

"Before you start agai-" Too late, an open hand met his cheek.

"Why did you want to talk to me?" Violet was struggling to keep what composure she still had.

"Maybe, if you let me talk without hitting me, I'll have time to get to that."

Violet shut the door and stood beside it, her arms crossed, holding them against her ribs.

***

Diana could hear the conversation when they weren't whispering, which they almost never were. One of the housekeeper's laughed when they saw that Diana was leaning against the door listening in, and Diana had to shush her to listen. She had known the boy wanted to talk to Violet, but he wouldn't say why. Now she knew.

***

"Okay," the boy started. "I'm sure you remember me due to your reaction, but maybe not my name. My name is Taivna, I'm an Elf. You could probably tell from my ears." The boy's hands were shaking too much to hide, "I wanted to start off with 'I'm sorry for what happened' again, but you kind of hit me and I'm not really sure I want to talk anymore, so, if you don't mind, I've changed my mind and I'm going to leave."

The boy reached around Violet trying to get at the doorknob. Violet stepped in front of it. "You asked to talk to me, so what is it you wanted to talk about then?" Taivna got the message, he wasn't leaving until he talked.

The boy started fidgeting with his thumbs. "Well, since I work at Heidskun, I've noticed you around a few times. You're being kept here, right?"

"What's your point?"

"Well, I wanted to give you something, to help pass the time." The boy started searching through his pockets. "Oh, where is it," the boy whispered to himself. "Ah! There it is!" Taivna took a stone out of his pocket, it was about the size of his palm. It was shimmering with all sorts of colors.

"It's... a rock?" Violet was puzzled. The boy wanted to give her a rock? How could she pass the time with a rock? She hadn't been sure what to expect, but she definitely wasn't expecting a rock.

"It's more than just a rock. I found it in the riverbed; it's a special kind of stone. Let me show you." The boy took the stone back from Violet's hand and walked over to a fountain in the corner of the room. Dipping the rock into the water, it changed to blue.

"So, it's a rock that changes color?" That was more interesting, but still not a time killer.

"Hold on." The boy walked back to Violet, "Stick out your arm."

Violet did just that. The boy took her hand in his, and dragged the rock across the back of her hand, leaving a trail of blue. "See?"

Violet was pleasantly surprised, but was also a little annoyed with the boy. "Why did you test it on my hand?"

"I don't know, I didn't have anything else!"

"What about your own hand, genius?"

"I don't know! I didn't think about it!"

"You don't think too much do you? It better come off!" She started rubbing at the back of her hand, and it spread to her other hand.

"You're getting off course here, the point isn't your hand; the point is that it can create color."

"More than just blue, I would hope."

"Of course it can! You just need a different temperature of water, which shouldn't be a problem for you since you have a bath."

"I'm surprised you even noticed the bath, sicko."

The boy blushed a bit. "It doesn't leave marks on your skin either, which is good." He ignored her remark.

"Unless you purposely draw on it." Violet said, taking the stone and marking the boy's cheek.

The boy stood looking at the stone for a bit before letting out a sigh. "Well, hopefully you can pass some time with drawing."

"Do you want the stone back at some point?" Violet asked.

"No, the stone is a gift. It's for you, so keep it. Well, I should get back to work." The boy walked to the door.

Violet felt happy, primarily because he had thought about her and had got her something, even if it was a rock. Violet gave Taivna a hug, "Thanks for the stone," she told him, marking his other cheek with it and letting out a giggle.

"I'm glad you like it." He said with a sigh. "At this rate, I'll regret giving it to you by tomorrow."

The boy opened the door, and left. Diana moved into the doorway after the boy had gone by, looking back at him. "Why was his face blue?" she asked, already knowing the answer.

"He gave me a coloring rock." Violet said, trying to suppress a smile.

"That's kind of him. I guess you will need something to draw on, hm?"

"Yeah." Violet was still staring at the rock. "Did you already know what he wanted?" She looked up at Diana.

Diana only shrugged.

Chapter Twenty One
Quiet Days

The house had been very quiet since the accident, and it unnerved Peter. He was used to having someone there when he got home, or to get home at the same time as his sister, but since she was in the hospital, he went home alone, and was alone once he got home. His mother had spent every day at the hospital for the last month, and it wasn't for work anymore, and his father had to work extra hours to make ends meet while his mother was taking time off. Often times he would not even see his father until late at night, and he would be going to sleep when he got home anyways.

Peter would be lying if he said he liked having the house to himself, and he would also be lying if he said he didn't miss his sister. Even if he found her unbearable, he still liked having her around. Peter tried to be upset about the little things to take his mind off of the bigger things, like how he hadn't gotten to go to the zoo with his family.

Peter's father usually left him a note to let him know there was food in the fridge, or some money on the table to order something in.

Peter and his father went to the hospital once a week, to give his mom some company, and to check up on Violet. Her condition never changed, she was always still in a coma with no signs of change. The only development were the cuts and bruises healing. When they went to the hospital, Peter was often left alone in the room with his sister, because his parents had to talk outside and they didn't want him to hear. If it made him worry, he didn't want to hear anyways.

Peter was often asked at school about his sister, but he didn't want to talk about it. Some of Violet's senior friends would come to him sometimes to ask him how she was, and he could only ever answer with the same "I don't know" which made him so sad that he had to fight back tears every time someone asked. School helped keep him distracted at least; he wanted to stay there most days so he wouldn't have to go back home to his isolation, but now that summer had arrived, he was confined to his home most days for even longer periods of isolation.

Peter's only three times of reprieve were when he was playing on his computer, when he was at school, and when he was sleeping, for he had never been a night dreamer; it was day dreams that he had.

This night was like any other, he was home alone in the living room, playing a game on his computer with the T.V. on. His father got home at the same time as always, eleven in the evening, but he did not say anything to Peter this time. His father went straight up the stairs to his room without a word.

Peter knew better than to press; his father rarely cried, and he was better left alone when he did.

Chapter Twenty Two
The Final Gathering

The different races had come together near the lake in preparation for the war. The shore was wide and left room still between the army and the trees. There were people around the whole perimeter of the lake, and in the lake. The Phoenix was overhead giving light to the communion. Diana had informed Hestaphal the week prior that the Denizens had started gathering at the swamp, they must have been preparing for war. The Denizens were a day's journey away now, and the northern races were ready and waiting.

Hestaphal was sitting among his colleagues of the Guild. Archibald stood up from the crowd of shapeshifters.

"Can everyone hear me?" He said out loud, standing up. He only stood slightly taller than the others who were sitting.

Various responses came from his audience.

"Yeah"

"Loud and clear"

"Go ahead, Archie"

"A little louder if you could"

"Ok," he says, raising his voice a bit, "I just wanna give a quick speech for ye all." He ran a hand through his thinning hair. "So, the Denizens are gonna be here tomorrow, and we'll have to start fighting. I just want to tell ye all, I have enjoyed teaching every single one o' ye, and if any o' us fall, I know it will be a very heavy weight on each o' our hearts. So don't put me through that!" He shouted jokingly, pointing a finger at the crowd and earning a quiet chuckle from them. "But honestly, truly I have faith in ye all. Together, with the help of these lovely people," He said, gesturing with his arms to the other groups around the lake, "We can win this war. Those damned savages will regret the day they tried to take our land!"

This earned a cheer from the crowd.

Across the lake, the Gnomes were setting up war machines. Over a dozen had already been prepared, and many more lay in piles waiting to be built. The mayor was walking between construction teams, surveying their work. He had promised each worker a fair pay for their efforts, but he wanted good work for it. Baird was among the working crew, with his son Guile. Baird had been appointed as foreman for his construction group, but it only seemed fair in his mind that he help, and not just give advice or directions.

The Elves were neighboring the Gnome workers, and they were much more etiquette and tolerable than the Dwarves on the other side of them. The Elves sat in small groups, leaving room to walk between them, and were listening to songs from some of their brothers. Their songs were mostly instrumental, being put on by a select few who had brought lutes. Every now and then a song had vocals in it, and those lines were taken up by the Elf women in the crowds.

The Dwarves were much more unpleasant to be near than the Elves. One Dwarf was playing an instrument that resembled an accordion, putting on a quick tune for the other Dwarves, who were all standing and dancing, cheering and laughing. They were loud and obnoxious, all carrying a mug of ale in one hand and someone else in their other. The noise from the Dwarves could be heard from across the lake. They compensated for the lack of sound from the other groups around the lake.

In the lake, the Capricorns were playing a game involving a ball of water that they made using their aquamancy. They had to keep the water together while passing it to each other, whoever let the ball collapse into the lake lost the game. Losing did not matter much, for they started a new round as soon as the first ended. Pricus was asleep at the bottom of the lake, preserving his energy, as he had told his children to do.

The Sea Folk had just begun to arrive. A whirlpool had formed on the surface of the lake, opposite the Capricorns, and Mermaids and Mermen alike were pouring forth from it. Some carried tridents, other's held staves. The Queen came through last, her daughter Miulein at her side. They both carried staves. The Queens staff was silver with a blue spherical stone at the center. The stone had rippling lines running across its surface, looking like the waves on an ocean. Her daughter's staff was silver as well, but it bore a purple stone instead; its surface was frosted over like a glacier.

The sky below the Phoenix was filled with Fairies. They were mingling with each other in flocks of colored wings and practicing their magic. They had already been told by the Dryads where they were needed, and where they would go after the final gathering. The Dryads would be waiting at those spots.

The Centaurs had the largest area to themselves, they had requested a wide open grassy area so they could keep their legs stretched and so they could race. They had set up some training dummies to practice sword handling against as well. They were not fully interested in the festivities of the final gathering; they wanted to be prepared for the battles to come.

Diana had stayed at Heidskun, she felt a responsibility towards Violet, as though she had to keep her company during the war. She had spent time with Violet when she had first tried the stone for drawing. They had decided to set up a canvas in the washroom, since the bath was located there as well and they needed the water from it.

The only one who had yet to arrive was The Gazer himself. Hestaphal had not lost hope in him, no matter how many times others had asked him where The Gazer was. "He will be here," he simply replied, and that was the end of it.

The gathering was approaching its end, they would soon sleep until the early morning, when they would make their final preparations for the battle.

The leaders of each group made a final speech to their people, raising moral and giving confidence to them. Hestaphal gave a final reassuring speech to everyone as a whole, telling them that The Gazer had promised he would arrive when he was needed most.

The Phoenix had gone to sleep, marking the end of the festivities. It slept as an egg, floating in a cradle of fire above the water.

Everyone had begun to pass into sleep, but Hestaphal stayed awake for a while, looking up at the sky. He noticed a group of stars in the shape of a serpent, moving together in the sky, high above the clouds. Before he finally closed his eyes, he heard a voice say "I am here" and his mind was at ease.

Chapter Twenty Three
Hope

Today marked the end of the second month since Violet had fallen into a coma. Diana had spent every day by her side, reading her stories, sharing memories and sleeping to pass the time. Violet's subtle reactions had become a common event, and because of that, they had lost their value to Diana. She needed to see progress being made, she needed to know it was still making a difference.

The other doctors had started to look at Diana the way she used to look at people in her situation; it was that look a pity. Diana had started to get teary eyed more often, but she still managed to suppress any noise. Diana could still not bring herself to go home. Violet's cuts had completely healed over, not a scratch was on her body.

It tore at Diana's heart, the fact that she could be beside someone for two months but never hear a word from them. The doctors were trying to ease her pain, while at the same time trying to make the idea that Diana may never hear from her daughter again seem normal. Diana would not let her hope wane. She refused to think of losing her daughter, but deep in her heart, she worried.

Chapter Twenty Four
Home Sick

Violet was in the observatory, watching the northern races hold their final festival. Diana was with her. They watched as the party came to its peak, and watched as it died down and when they eventually all slept. When Violet was about to go look somewhere else, she noticed stars come into view. It was impossible that so many stars could be so low to the ground, let alone one. The stars moved out of view, and Violet turned to Diana. "What was that?"

"That, my dear, was The Gazer. Very few people have seen The Gazer, and they would not assume that to be him, it conceals him from those who would seek him out. He has not broken his word, he waits for the battle to begin."

"He's a bunch of stars?"

"Sort of." Diana answered, a smile appearing on her face. "You'll see him soon enough."

"It could never come quick enough." Violet said, setting her elbows down on the stone circle.

Diana's expression changed quicker than it had before, she looked hurt. "Do you not like it here?"

Violet had not thought of what she said before she had said it. "Oh, no, no. That's not it at all. I really like being here, especially meeting everyone. It's just that I miss my home."

Diana turned to go up the stairs. "I understand. I will give you some privacy." And she left up the stairs.

Violet felt terrible. She hadn't meant to hurt Diana's feeling. She became upset with herself.

She returned to the picture of the full map before leaving the observatory. She took the rock from her sleeve, taking note of her still marked hand. The blue would not come off of her skin no matter what she did. What an idiot that boy could be. But she grinned whenever she thought about having marked his face. He must look silly with that still showing on his skin so visibly.

Violet returned to her room, going straight to the washroom and drawing the bath full of water. She always found that when she drew with the rock, it calmed her. She had been working on the same picture since she got the rock. She struggled to remember its details, but she had put a lot of effort into drawing her house, and it was almost done.

A knock came from the door to her bedroom, faintly audible from the washroom. "Come in!" Violet called. Footsteps came to the doorway of the washroom. Violet turned to see Taivna, his cheeks still faintly colored blue. He had brought towels again.

"Were you hoping for a repeat?" Violet teased him, while suppressing a laugh from seeing the marks.

"No, I'm just doing what I was told. That looks nice, what is it?"

Violet set the rock on the ledge of the easel. "It's my house from where I used to live."

"It looks very nice. I can tell you put a lot of effort into it."

A single tear ran down Violet's cheek. "Thanks." Violet didn't like talking about home, it made her sad and it hurt to think about. "Shouldn't you be at war?"

"I'm still too young to be allowed to join the army. You have to have seen your eighteenth set of seasons, I am almost finished witnessing my seventeenth."

"So that would make you almost seventeen?" Violet clarified.

"My people typically don't use years for distinguishing age, but yeah, I would be seventeen in a few months."

Violet stood up from her stool, and walked over to Taivna. "Thanks for the towels." And she set them on the shelf beside the sink. She returns to her stool, glancing back at the doorway before sitting down, and noticing Taivna was still stood in it, looking at the floor. "Taivna?"

"Yes?" His neck straightened once more.

"Are you waiting for something?"

"Kind of... I mean, no!" The boy's cheeks flushed red beneath the blue. "I'll go, sorry for wasting your time."

"No, wait!" Violet called, but it was too late. The boy had already ran from the room. He would be too embarrassed to come back even if he had heard her. Violet sat back on the stool, leaning her back against the bath. "Oh, you idiot!" She muttered to herself. "He was letting you in, but instead you shut the door on him. Great, just great."

"I met Taivna on the stairwell," Diana said to Violet. Violet, surprised as she was that someone was there, fell over with the stool. "He looked a bit upset. Are you okay?"

"My god! Would it kill you to knock?!" Violet asked while pulling herself off of the floor.

"Sorry, I just figured you wouldn't mind talking." Diana walked over to Violet, picking the stool up from the ground and setting it on its feet. "So?"

"So what?"

"Do you want to talk? About the boy, maybe?"

Violet sat down on the floor with her knees up to her chin. "I'm such a screw up. There's no way I'll get another chance like that. He opened the door, and I closed it on him."

"So you said." Diana walked over to Violet. "Get up, Violet, there are much better places to talk from than on the floor." Diana stuck out her hand for Violet, who took it. "Come with me, dear. We can talk more in my room."

Violet gave no objection. She followed Diana further up the mother tree, stopping at one of the last rooms before the top. Diana entered the room, holding the curtain aside for Violet to come through as well.

Violet had not seen Diana's room before. "A lot of green, don't you think?"

"Judging my room when I'm here to help you? That's rather rude, don't you think? And for the record, I quite like the green." Diana crossed the room, removing a slightly taller stool than the one in front of her mirror and placing it behind the shorter one. She sat upon the taller one with a brush in hand. "Well? Come on! Your hair isn't going to brush itself, my girl."

Violet sat down on the front stool, and let Diana run the brush through her hair. "So?" Diana started, "You like this boy, don't you?"

"Yeah, I guess." Violet felt mopey thinking about it.

"Well, if you guess, then you must not like him very much. So why are you so bothered by him if you don't like him?"

"Yeah, okay, I do like him. I just wish I could handle myself better around him."

"How do you mean?"

"Well, when I see him I feel really awkward in my own skin. I feel like I need to impress him or something, but when I do that then I make a fool of myself. I don't know why I feel that way though. How come I can't just act normal around him?"

"My dear, love does that, it makes you feel silly. Listen to me now, okay? If the boy likes you back, you won't have to impress him. If he really likes you, no matter what you do, he'll still like you, so just be yourself. You say that you don't know how to act normal when you're near him, but all you have to do, my dear, is treat him like a normal person. That's all he is after all, a normal person, okay? If it's meant to be, then it will be, so lighten up a bit, would you?"

Diana continued to run the comb through Violet's hair, straightening knots and removing twigs and leaves. It brought comfort to Violet, helping with Diana's words to calm her mind. Tears started to run down Violet's cheeks. She missed her family, her home, her friends, but most of all, she missed her mother.

"Oh, my girl! Don't cry, please! Everything is going to be okay, I assure you." Violet spun around on the stool, burying her face in Diana's dress and wrapping her arms around her, searching for comfort. Diana put one arm around Violet, and ran the other through her hair, whispering reassurances to her.

Chapter Twenty Five
The First Battle

Hestaphal woke up. He stood up from the grass and looked around the lake. No one was awake yet, except for the trees.

"Shapeshifter, we must speak with you." The voice came from his mind.

"What is it you would like to say?" Hestaphal answered.

"The Dryads have been gone scouting the whole night, they returned early this morning, reporting that the enemy approaches quickly. They will be upon us within two hours. You must wake the others; preparations must be made quickly."

Hestaphal was surprised by this news. Did the Denizens not sleep? How could they possibly be so near? "Thank you, I will wake them immediately. Thank the Dryads for me as well."

"We will convey your message to them, shapeshifter. Fight well."

Hestaphal awoke Archibald. "Heh? What is it, boy?" The Dwarf was still groggy.

"The trees have given me a warning; the Denizens will be here within two hours, we must wake everyone." Hestaphal told him.

Archibald's eyes widened, "So soon? The sun is barely touching the sky."

"Yes, but we must wake the others immediately. I will go around the left of the lake, you go to the right. We must make haste."

The two went their own direction, spreading the word. They started out by waking groups of people, but quickly started shouting it out. "Everyone up! The Denizens will be here soon! We must be ready!"

Within minutes the beach was alive with movement, everyone was gathering their tools of war. The water too was covered in ripples from the commotion beneath its surface. The Phoenix ascended once more into the sky, its light pouring out onto the meadows and forests around it.

Hestaphal took to the skies as a raven once more, seeing the dust rising from the horizon. The Denizens would arrive soon. Hestaphal returned to the ground, making his own preparations. He looked to the sky. The sun had almost erased all of the stars from the sky, but a select few still glimmered, a cluster of stars was included in those select few. The cluster appeared to be moving, and Hestaphal knew the morning battle would go in their favor.

"Formations!" Archibald was getting the army into position. In the lake, a group of Capricorn aquamancers created a pillar of water for others to float in, so that they could see farther. Pricus and the Queen of the Sea Folk were among the ones who were on the pillar. The Denizens could be seen on the horizon from the ground now.

The army was in position. The Denizens came to a halt, leaving three hundred meters between the two armies. A charcoal skinned Troll rode into the center of the battlefield atop a Manticore. The Manticore had green fur with a black tinge.

Whispers ran through the northern army, "Kenghala? The terror of the lake? How did the Denizens come to have him?"

"Send your leader forward!" The Troll shouted, his voice commanded obedience.

Archibald started forward, but Hestaphal caught his shoulder, "Let me go in your stead. It would be a much more devastating blow to lose you than myself." And before Archibald could answer Hestaphal had started forward.

Hestaphal took the form of a Unicorn and went to speak with the Troll.

"You are their leader?" The Troll chieftain asked, his voice quieter, speaking only to Hestaphal now.

They were equal distances between their armies, and stood nearly thirty feet from each other.

"Yes. My name is Hestaphal of the Guild of Transformation, surpassed only by our teacher Archibald. What is your name, fellow leader?"

"Do not treat this like a gathering between friends, shapeshifter, the war has already begun, this is but a formality. My name is Trygon, descendant of the great Chieftain Terigorn, slayer of Kairenax Wilthren, the last leader of Man. My people come on this day to bring the reckoning of six centuries of crimes to the northern races. Today we will return to our ancestral lands."

"Trygon, I would ask that you reconsider this war. My people are prepared to welcome you into the northern lands once more. We ask for your forgiveness for the past transgressions of our ancestors, and we forgive your people for the transgressions of their ancestors."

The Troll turned his Manticore, ready to return to his army. "Know this, shapeshifter. Before this war is finished, your head will be hanging above my throne as I watch the mother tree of Heidskun burn, and your soul will be fuel for Kenghala. I will enjoy every moment of your death, and I will make it very slow, and very painful."

"No matter the outcome of this war, your people will be welcomed to their ancestral lands. I can only hope that you will not hold vengeance in your heart from this defeat."

Trygon spat on the ground before Hestaphal, and returned to his Denizens, a roar coming from Kenghala. Hestaphal galloped back to the northern army.

Archibald met Hestaphal at the front ranks, "Well? What did he say?"

"He is adamant that this war must be fought." Hestaphal marched along the front of the army. "Races of the Northern army! We are here today to fight a war that will change history! Fight to your last breath and victory will be assured! Do not let fear consume you! Let the enemy come to you! They are stronger, but what they have over us in strength, we surpass them by in agility and intellect!"

Trygon was rallying his troops as well. "Denizens of the Southern Marshes! We have come to the doorstep of the northern lands today to reclaim what our ancestors lost centuries ago! We will crush the enemy and burn their villages! We will wipe them from history itself! None can stand before us! Charge!"

Throngs of creatures poured forth from the Denizen army. The structure of their ranks collapsed with the beginning of the first battle; they no longer cared for systematic formations, for they sought to collect a debt in blood, each member taking their own path towards the enemy.

The northern army held fast, their ranks tightened and the Centaurs raised great shields, bracing themselves for the incoming onslaught.

The first to arrive from the southern army were the Goblins. They were quick on their feet and ran faster than the other races, charging towards the shields. They collided with the metal barricade, knives bouncing off its surfaces. The Goblins threw their bodies at the front line, landing on their backs in the grass, and were crushed by their own army as the next line approached.

Next to arrive were the Trolls, their long legs carrying them quickly. The Trolls stood tall, their heads visible over the shields.

"Fire!" A signal from Archibald, a volley of arrows fell upon the Denizens as the Elves let go of their strings.

A few Trolls still stood, but were quickly skewered by spears from the Centaurs, giving the shield wall a moment of respite. Minotaurs were approaching next, alongside a few Cyclopes and Ogres. The brute force of their army.

Most of the Minotaurs wielded two headed axes, while some carried flails. The Cyclopes mostly carried small trees that still were still adorned with their roots and branches. A few Cyclops carried boulders. Overhead, Trolls atop winged Chimeras flew towards the northern army.

"Someone stop those boulder throwing bastards!" Archibald yelled to the back lines. He then pulled Hestaphal down to him, "Where's The Gazer? You said he would be here when he was needed, but he is not here."

"Look to the sky, Archibald, do you not see stars in the morning sky? He is here, but he waits until he is needed most." Hestaphal answered. "Shapeshifters! Bring the Chimeras down!" He shouted before taking to the sky as a raven to join the Phoenix in the air. Once he was far enough above the army, he transformed into a Griffin, colliding with a Chimera and knocking its rider into the trees below.

Dozens of winged beasts took to the sky from the northern army. There were Griffins, horned Pegai, giant hawks, and a single ebon quilled Hippogriff. The Dwarves moved up to fill the gaps where the shapeshifters had been.

From the lake, spears of water flew through the air, puncturing the bodies of the Cyclopes before exploding into needles. The last few Cyclopes carrying boulders threw them into the shield wall, making holes in a few spots in the wall that were quickly mended with new shields. The Minotaurs charged the shield wall on all fours, throwing their weapons ahead into the northern ranks, impaling their foes and pinning them to the ground. "Break ranks!" The order went out among the shield bearers. The Centaurs scrambled to make way for the oncoming Minotaurs. Most succeeded while some could not make way quick enough and were carried back, gored by the Minotaurs' horns. The Minotaurs halted their charge, recovering their weapons from either corpses or dying soldiers and swinging at the Dwarves of the middle ranks. The Minotaurs rang havoc among the middle ranks as they approached the Elvin archers. Their slow assault was ceased once the Sea Folk froze their limbs with ice magic, making them vulnerable to the heads of Dwarven hammers.

The shield wall repaired itself before the Cyclopes and Ogres could pass through. The Centaurs held them at bay with spears and with the aid of the aquamancers of the lake.

The onslaught spilled forth from the southern army, countless creatures charging the northern blockade to meet their end. Dozens of Goblins took to the trees with the plan of flanking the northern ranged military, but met their demise by the roots of the forest, being buried beneath the dirt of the forest floor. The Denizens learned quickly not to enter the trees. They continued for hours to pile against the blockade, meeting their ends by steel or by water.

The Minotaurs charged the shield wall once more, but it carried worse results than the first time. The Minotaurs were struck down before they reached the shield wall by the water lances of the Capricorns.

The battlefield was ridden with corpses and the blood of the fallen. The fight carried on until the sun was setting, numerous tactics being attempted and repeated with no great results.

"Retreat!" Trygon called out to his army. "Savor this victory, northern weaklings! Tomorrow will bring your demise!" The Denizens retreated over the horizon, Trygon was the last to go.

The northern army celebrated their victory despite the damper. Before the sun fully set, they gathered the bodies of their fallen comrades, bringing them to the farthest end of the lake. They cleared the battlefield of enemy corpses as well, sorting them in groups by race. On this occasion, victory tasted sour.

Chapter Twenty Six
A Bird's Eye View

Violet focused the Observatory on the Lake of Lenidral, bearing witness to the atrocities of war. The grass was stained red with blood, and the outskirts of the battlefield were littered with corpses. There were hundreds of dead, piled high in groups; they bore similarities to the others of their pile.

Diana was beside Violet. She informed Violet of what race each pile was. "The pile with the most dead, closest to the trees here, those are Goblins. Beside them, the ones with the long limbs, you have seen them before; they're the Trolls. The large bodied beige ones beside them are Ogres. The one eyed beings are Cyclopes; you have seen them as well. The horned ones are Minotaurs, I believe you might know them as well, they are easy to distinguish. And the winged beasts, those are Chimeras."

"They remind me of the Manticores."

The Chimeras hardly resembled the Manticores. The ones that she saw now looked like a lion with wings and the horns of a bull, while the Manticores had the tail of a scorpion and the hind legs of a goat.

Diana glanced at Violet briefly, then looked back to the Observatory, "Faintly, I suppose. Let us see the northern casualties. They are few, I hope." They found the fallen northern soldiers near the lake. The casualties were mostly Centaurs. A few Dwarves laid among them, some cut in two from the Minotaurs' axes, and two Elves lay among the dead. Diana scanned the bodies quickly for anyone she recognized, but saw none. "Perhaps we should not stare upon the dead. It is not a sight I would like to remember."

Violet attempted to return to the map, but the Observatory would not unfocus. A voice filled Violet's mind as the Observatory was filled with white light.

"What is this? The Human girl?" The voice was calm, but carried power. "More than just the Human girl, the Queen of Nymphs as well. It is as I expected, she resides at Heidskun." The light changed from white to blue. "You are fortunate that I have agreed to fight alongside the northern army." There was a long pause. "Speak, Human."

Words escaped Violet, she turned to Diana, who appeared to be oblivious of the voice.

"She does not see what you see, and she does not hear me either. Speak, and she will not hear you. To her, time is standing still, but she does not know that."

"Are you The Gazer? Hestaphal said that you can send me home. Is that true?"

The light changed green. "Yes, I can return you to where you belong, but the shapeshifter has charged me with his war. I cannot help you until he is satisfied. Combat drains much of my energy, so I must wait for a crucial moment. If I was to fight the whole duration, I would have no energy to return you home for many months."

"Will the war end quickly?"

"No war lasts as long as another; I cannot say when you will be returned home. It is in the hands of the northern army."

"How did you notice that we were watching?"

"This contraption of yours uses crude magic. To the trained eye, however, the user is easily noticed. It is because of the Observatory that I can speak to you now. However, I must go; take solace in the fact that you will return home. Until next we meet, Violet Glendale."

"No, wait!" Violet shouted.

Diana recoiled from the Observatory, caught by surprise with Violet's sudden shouting. "What is it?"

"Did you not hear him at all?"

"Hear who?"

"Ugh, whatever." Violet felt silly now, but she was also upset that The Gazer could not stay longer. "I'll tell you later; I'm going back upstairs." Violet walked to the stairs and started up them.

Diana stayed standing by the observatory for a moment before following, put off by Violet's sudden change of attitude. She returns to the world map, and follows Violet up the stairs.

Chapter Twenty Seven
Change in Tactics

The morning of the second day broke over the battlefield, and with it, the Denizens over the horizon. The northern ranks were already in position. The dim sky was lit up by torchlight. The Denizens had brought torches. A wave of fire marched towards the frontier.

"They're gonna burn the whole bloody forest down!" Archibald shouted. "They're forcing our hand, we can't stay here if they burn the trees. We have to take the fight to them."

Most of the Centaurs returned their shield to their camp and gathered new weapons; swords, maces, axes and bows. Some still carried their shields and spears.

"Everyone! We're gonna have to fight on the battlefield! If they burn this forest down, then we'll have already lost!" Archibald shouted to the northern army.

Hestaphal was watching the sky, a few stars still glimmered from the night, but there also remained the moving cluster. He had faith.

"Hestaphal!" Archibald shouted at him. "Get yer head outta the stars! Ye and the rest of the Guild will join me in the sky to cover for the other forces."

"As you wish, Archibald." Hestaphal answered.

A horn sounded from the Denizens. The second battle would soon begin.

The northern army formed a line along the forest. "This battle will be just like the last!" Archibald was giving a speech. "We're gonna send them back over that hill before the sun sets! Their torches are gonna lay in the mud along with their dead! The northern army is superior in every manner, and today we will prove it once more! Take heart, brothers and sisters of the north; they ain't seen nothin' yet!" A cheer ran through the line along with the metallic clatter of sword on shield.

A horn rang out over the battlefield again. Their enemies would soon arrive. The marching Denizens broke into a sprint with the final blow of the horn.

"Meet them in the field!" Archibald called out, and the northern army rushed to meet them.

Trygon rode atop Kenghala at the front of the southern army, axe in hand. Before the armies collided, Trygon leapt from his Manticore into the northern army, landing among Dwarves, and cleaving his surrounding foes with his axe in a circular sweep. The charcoal skinned Troll stood taller than the Centaurs, and the head of his axe was wider than the Dwarves he had slain with it. Kenghala followed his rider into the fray, landing atop a Centaur and splitting it in two. His scorpion tail impaled a Dwarf, leaving a gaping hole in his midsection.

Most of the Denizens dropped their torches on the battlefield, leaving the fire to spread across the battlefield.

The battle broke into chaos, the northern and southern forces fought each other with a lust for blood. Water artillery was being fired from the lake far into the oncoming Denizen forces, thinning their reinforcements as the battle raged. A group of Goblins still held their torches and were making for the forest on the edge of the battlefield. Their torches met the first trees as the Dryads appeared from the tree line, sending a volley of razor sharp leaves through the Goblin pack. Each cut left a stinging pain and a bleeding cut. The leaves circled back time and time again until the Goblins lay in a heap of bloodstained corpses, disfigured with thousands of small cuts across their entire body.

The fire from the torches caught in the grass of the tree line. A swarm of water sprites came from the canopy of surrounding trees, dousing the flames that encroached upon the forest with water before the fire could spread further.

Cyclopes were throwing boulders into the fray, crushing both friend and foe with their reckless tactics.

Fire sprites flew down from the sky towards the battlefield. They worked together to manipulate the fire that was burning all across the battlefield. They collected the flames into a miniature sun above the battlefield, and threw it into the back line of the Denizens.

A hail of boulders and giant arrows crashed into the Denizens' reinforcements. The Gnomes were firing their war machines, aided in the reloading process by volunteer Dwarves.

The sky above the Denizens started to fill with Chimeras, giant bats that had acid spilling from their maws down to the ground, and several monstrous Wyverns. The Wyverns were amalgamations. They looked like snakes with wings, but they had clawed limbs hanging below them as well. Their heads were that of a bearded vulture, but on a much larger scale, and their scales were interlaced with feathers. Their tales ended in a cluster of quills. The Wyverns were all brown, with white at the tips of their feathers.

The Guild of Transformation took to the sky. The Wyverns were too strong for them however; their hide could not be pierced by their talons or their horns. They switched their focus, targeting the giant bats and the Chimeras, leaving the Wyverns for the Phoenix and the Sea Folk. They each took their own target. Hestaphal focused on one of the giant bats. Its acid could cause serious damage if it was to touch any part of his body, so he would have to be very careful.

The bat's rider carried a spear that reached nearly eight feet. The Troll jabbed at Hestaphal whenever he tried to attack, forcing him to keep his distance. A cry came from the battlefield below. One of the bats had landed in the middle of the warring armies, erupting into a geyser of green acid melting both ally and enemy. Closer to the lake, one of the bats dove down into the raging battle without having been struck down. They were living bombs!

"Shapeshifters! Don't let the bats anywhere near the battle! Take them from the sky and let them fall into the Denizens!" The northern aerial assault changed target, their priority was now the bats. Nearly a dozen of the acid filled air rodents still flew in the skies.

Four groups of Sea Folk were formed in the lake. They focused their magic into giant icicles, aiming for the Wyverns. Volleys of four soared through the air towards the Wyverns. Two Wyverns were struck down on the first volley, but the Wyverns quickly adapted to the new threat. They avoided the icicles, bending their serpentine bodies around the projectiles path. The Phoenix tore through the Wyverns who could evade the icicles, splitting them open with searing claws and boiling their blood with white fire.

Trygon was paving through the northern forces as his army fell around him. While his people may not be superior in combat, they had numbers. The charcoal Troll had several broken arrow shafts protruding from his body, but they seemed to not affect him in the slightest. He continued clearing a path through the northern army, his axe red with blood and his eyes burning with death's lust.

"Fall back! Assemble the shield wall!" An order from Archibald, he had suffered a blow to his right leg that gave him a limp when he walked. He was fortunate that he had the ability to fly if he needed to.

All of the Centaurs fled to the camp, collecting their shields and forming a wall at the opening to the lake. The Dwarves and Elves retreated behind the shield wall.

The northern army formed ranks once more, the Elves collecting their bows and quivers once more and setting their glaives in the ground. They fired a volley into the encroaching southern forces, followed by a rain of needle shaped ice from the Sea Folk.

"Fall back, Denizens! Do not fight them where they would hope to fight you, they try to lure you into the same fate as your fallen brothers. Let today be remembered as our first victory of many over the northern scum! Tomorrow we will end this once and for all!"

And with that, the southern army fled over the horizon once more, leaving the battlefield scarred with fire and blood and littered with corpses.

Chapter Twenty Eight
War Casualties

Violet and Diana had witnessed the whole battle, and now looked at the result. Bodies lay mangled across the entire field. The grass was nothing but black strands on a charcoal field. Violet felt as if she was going to vomit. She was not, by any means, used to seeing such realistic gore. At least in movies she knew it was fake. The most exposure she had to such sights was her Biology class where they had dissected toads, but the dissection still made her queasy despite being on a much smaller scale.

Death always came as a shock to young people. How could life end when it had only just begun?

Violet came to a realization when she saw all of these bodies. Right now, in her own world, she was pretty much like them; she was in a deep sleep that held her so tight that she might as well be dead for how little she could do. She probably couldn't even breathe on her own. That is, if she was still alive. The thought made Violet stricken with fear. Could it be possible she was dead? What if this was what her afterlife was? Fear enveloped her once more. It had been over two months now since she had woken up in this world. Would she ever wake up? She couldn't hold it back anymore, she fell to her knees, gagging, but nothing came out. She felt as if she were drowning.

***

The hospital room had been quiet. Diana was alone with Violet, reading her a story. A noise came from Violet, and at first Diana was so very excited. Was her daughter waking up? But then the noise came again, and again, until finally Violet's oxygen mask was filled with a yellow fluid. Diana immediately took off Violet's mask, calling for a doctor while doing so. She was vomiting, but since her stomach was empty, only the acid was coming up. She propped Violet up, leaning her forward to drain her mouth and prevent the acid from causing serious damage.

Doctor Lindbel came into the room and immediately started helping Diana by patting Violet on the back to get as much out as possible.

Diana was whispering to Violet.

***

"What's wrong, Violet?" Diana asked, kneeling beside Violet. She was worried, but didn't know how to help. "You're going to be okay, Violet. Everything's going to be okay."

Violet was still on her knees, her back lurching from time to time. She couldn't breathe, and she couldn't speak. She didn't know why.

***

After almost an hour of cleaning up the acid and keeping Violet sat up, Diana finally let her daughter lay back down. Diana and Lindbel had finally deemed it to be safe, because it had been nearly ten minutes since Violet had last gagged. They had had to slip on the oxygen mask from time to time to make sure Violet wouldn't asphyxiate, but finally, it was safe.

"Although that was a frightening episode, it is also reassuring. Her body is regaining motor control. She wouldn't have her gag reflex otherwise. Her condition is getting better." The Doctor explained.

"Thank you, Lindbel." Diana said. Once she was alone, she found her cheeks were damp, but she couldn't tell whether the tears were caused by fear or joy.

***

Violet was struggling to catch her breath. Her knees were quivering and her arms were shaking. She was so afraid. She didn't understand what had just happened to her, but she felt as if she were going to die. "I-. I think I'm okay." She said to Diana as she lifted herself from the floor. "I think I need to lie down though."

"Come, let's get you to your room then."

***

The Dwarf King was laying in his tent, his three sons beside him. His health had worsened since the war had started, but he had managed to fight these last two days.

He would not be fighting tomorrow.

"Aldreit." He managed to say between coughs. His breath reeked of booze and rot. "You are my eldest... I bestow upon you... the crown of the mountain people." He removed the crown from his head, placing it in

~ 100 ~

the hands of his oldest son. "Do not fail me... my son. Your people will need you in the days to come." He turned to his next son. "Breitol... You will serve your brother... with loyalty. His word is now law... and you will enforce it... my boy..." He turned to his youngest son. "Gein... You must find your own path... I am sorry..."

His last breath left the tent in silent despair.

***

The Sea Folk's healers were busier than the day before, as the casualties had been much greater today. Many of the Merpeople were growing tired; they had used much of their energy through healing wounds. Many of the wounds were too severe to heal. They did what they could, but in the end, they feared it would not be enough.

The Mermaid Queen was at the bottom of the lake speaking with Pricus. "Do you have faith in the northern races? Our numbers are waning, and the Denizens will soon overwhelm us." She said nonchalantly, as if nothing mattered less to her.

Pricus was laying against the muddy floor of the lake. "No matter the losses of our allies, in the end we will be victorious. Have you watched the sky at night? Or even at midday for that matter?"

"I have not. Why do you ask?"

"The stars are moving, Silvayna. The Gazer has been here these past two days, watching, waiting. The right opportunity has yet to come. He has not abandoned us as the others believe."

The Mermaid Queen parted her pink hair to look above the water's surface. She spots a group of stars moving together in a line. "It has been a long time since I last saw him, yet he shines just as brightly as before. It's peculiar how I had not spotted him until now."

***

The Elf king sat beside his advisor. He watched the Sea Folk attempt to heal the wounded, but they were often incapable of healing the more serious of cases.

"My lord, what is it that troubles you?" Sikator asked.

"So many lives lost, and for what? An ancient hatred that has persisted through centuries. The Denizens have been fooled; their leader was offered a peaceful mending, and he refused. He has damned his people."

"Such are the ways of mortals, my lord. Their greatest fear is to be forgotten, and that is why they strive to create history. They should know better though; it is the winner who writes history, and the losers are remembered only for their misdeeds. This war will only form a new wound between our people."

***

Hestaphal's nostrils stung with the smell of burning flesh. The battlefield was a gruesome sight. Bodies had been charred to the bone, leaving nothing to be recognized. How could they take part in the festival of bells when nothing remained? It tore at his heart to see such a sight. So many loved ones gone and their families had no way of saying goodbye.

While the southern forces had suffered more losses, the northern army had taken a greater blow. Their army was not as great in size, and they all knew it. The Denizens had already lost two times as many warriors as the northern army consisted of, but the numbers made no difference. They needed to cut the head from the snake, otherwise this war would only end in defeat for them.

The bodies were too many in numbers for the northern army to clear, so they stayed on the field to rot and for the bones to be crushed under foot. Hestaphal had an idea at that moment. He spread the word among the willing to join him in the field.

Together, they cracked the bones in two and buried them in the ground, leaving the jagged ends sticking out from the ground to be stepped on by the Denizens. They started from the far side of the field and worked their way back, so as not to step on the broken bones themselves.

They finished in the dark of night and returned to camp to get what rest remained for them in the night. They struggled to find sleep when they finally laid their heads upon the ground. They had broken the remains of the dead, and the spirits of the fallen now haunted their thoughts. What punishment awaited them in the next life for this crime?

Chapter Twenty Nine
The Third day of War

The northern army was awake long before the sun had risen. They were training in close quarters combat with each other. They did not want to fight as they had yesterday, but if the need arose they preferred to be ready. Dreams of restless dead had kept most of them awake that night, their actions of the evening past did not sit well in their consciences.

Hestaphal was sitting among his colleagues of the Guild. Most of them were still capable, a few of them however had sustained serious damage. One of them had a broken leg, inflicted by the club of an Ogre. Another had a gash in his side from one of the bat riders' spears, but he insisted he could still fight. Archibald refused to sit. He had carved a cane overnight since he could not catch a wink of sleep, and now he leaned on it to compensate for his injured leg.

The horn of war rang in the distance over the horizon. The northern army formed ranks at the entrance to the lake once more. They waited for what seemed like ages to them, before finally a second call of the horn was heard in the distance. The enemy was nearing. Waiting anxiously, the northern army saw no one climb over the horizon. The ground began to rattle with intervals of silence in between. From over the hill, the silhouette of a head came into view. It was followed by another, and then another, and then a total of nine came into view, and a hulking body. The beast stood nearly twenty feet tall and was covered in Trolls.

"Hydra!" Came a call from the rear ranks of the northern army. The northern army became restless. How could they kill a Hydra? The beast would kill them all!

The final call of a horn rang through the air, followed by a monstrous shriek from each of the nine heads. The noise was deafening, even at this distance. It made the shields in the Centaurs' hands vibrate, sending a shiver through their bodies.

The Hydra had purple skin, and was plated in blue metal. It was covered in scars from whips, its will had been broken, and now it was being given the opportunity to let loose its wrath.

The beast slowed once it had reached the beginning of the jagged expanse of broken bones, but the bones had much less effect on it than they were having on the Ogres and Trolls. The Goblins were nimble and avoided the white spikes with ease, and the Minotaurs' hooves could not be pierced, but the Trolls did not see them in time and collapsed in the battlefield, being crushed underfoot by their allies. The Ogres were oblivious to the bones, and charged forward with bleeding feet, stumbling from time to time.

"We're gonna have to focus everything on it." Archibald was saying, more to himself than to the others.

"The Phoenix may be able to kill it alone." Hestaphal answered, but even he was doubtful.

"That's not a risk I'd be willing to take, given our circumstances. It's all or nothing. Who knows, maybe this is when we need the old guard most, eh?"

The group of stars were still above the battlefield, moving from time to time, but always overhead. "Perhaps." Hestaphal answered.

Another screech came from the beast. It was now close enough that the Sea Folk and Capricorns could reach it with their magic, but not quite close enough for the archers or machines of war.

A volley of projectile ice and water pierced the creatures hide, leaving holes and tears in its skin. The wounds leaked black goo that repaired the flesh, quickly healing the injuries.

"Hold yer fire!" Archibald shouted. "This isn't accomplishing anything! We need to focus fire on the heads for the Phoenix. Ye all should know that two heads grow back for every one that is cut off, unless ye can burn the wound."

A screech louder than any other sounded from the beast. The Phoenix had dove upon the Hydra, decapitating one of its heads with its claws and searing the wound shut with the same touch.

This set the Hydra into a bloodlust. It increased its pace, charging the northern shield wall. The Trolls riding on its back readied their weapons as the Hydra drew closer to the shield wall, leaping down into the northern army when they were finally in range.

The Hydra was struck with boulders from the war machines, and its legs were impaled with giant arrows from the ballistae. Its front legs gave way, slapping its remaining eight heads against the ground, and its body followed as the back legs collapsed as well. The heads lifted from the ground in a flurry of motion, snatching one of the Capricorns from the lake and knocking many of the Dwarves into the deep water.

"Don't get near it!" Archibald shouted. "It's as dangerous now as it was before!"

The beast could not stand, but its heads were flailing about, lashing out at anything and everything. The northern army had slain the Trolls and reestablished the shield wall to hold back the southern army. A group of Elven archers joined the Centaurs in holding back the Denizens.

A thought was heard by all of the northern army, "Stand back, little ones."

The ground started to shake, gradually increasing until it was knocking them to their hands and knees. Roots shot out of the ground and speared through the Hydra, provoking an ear splitting screech from all eight of its heads. The blood soaked roots wrapped around the beast's necks, dragging them closer to the ground, until finally they could no longer move nor make a sound.

"Fire! We need fire!" Archibald was shouting.

A swarm of flame sprites came from the surrounding trees, eager to help once more. They approached the Hydra heads, gesturing to a nearby Dwarf, it happened to be Aldreit. The sprites made a gesture that looked like they were chopping wood. The Dwarf got the idea. One by one, Aldreit chopped the heads off, and the sprites would seal the wound, until finally the beast lay dead in a heap of black and red ooze.

Pricus had Hestaphal bring him the dead Capricorn. It was Leira.

"Poor girl." Pricus said, "She was so excited to go to war. I told her it wasn't how she thought it would be. And now here she lies, the poor child."

"I am sorry, Pricus." Hestaphal answered.

"Thank you, Shapeshifter, but you have done nothing wrong. I must bring her home now though. I will return soon." Pricus enveloped Leira in a bubble and brought her through a whirlpool. The other Capricorns were hiding their tears in the lake water.

Chapter Thirty
The Decisive Battle

The day was not yet finished. Trygon had been watching from the hill as the Hydra swept through the northern army and towards the lake. He was sure of its victory even while it lay on the ground. Until the trees stepped in, and then he was furious. He removed his axe from the ground and started towards the northern forces.

His axe was dark red, stained with the blood of yesterday's victims. His eyes burned with a lust for blood. This victory would not be taken away from him, his people would not be sent back to those wretched swamps.

He charged across the battlefield; the bones stabbing into the soles of his feet did not faze him. The shield wall came closer, and he raised his axe, letting loose a yell from his throat. He swept with the axe, knocking one of the shields aside and creating an opening. He jumped through the wall into the northern army, followed by some of his troops.

They began to fight through the northern army. Trygon's allies fell quickly, but he continued to fight. He was sliced with swords, hacked with axes, and clubbed with hammers; nothing would flinch him.

In the sky, a group of stars began to shine brightly and grow larger. They were falling to the ground. Streaks of light followed each beacon as they began to swirl together, forming one larger star. The light became blinding as the star crashed into the ground in the middle of the southern army, sending blue and white flames outwards and leaving a crater in the battlefield. Hundreds of Denizens ran from the sides of the crater, their skin glowing with star fire as it peeled away their flesh. Any who had been hit directly by the stars were vaporized on contact. The crater was filled with the blinding white light. Smoke and dust rose from the crater as the light dimmed. The light changed to a blue, and from the crater the shape of a serpent crawled. The serpent was nearly transparent, its body defined only by the stars of its spine. The silhouette resembled a Dragon without wings. The body of the serpent shimmered into view, its scales glowing blue from the starlight beneath them.

The battlefield was still, all eyes were upon the astral Dragon. Whispers ran through both armies, "The Gazer..."

A booming voice rang out across the battlefield, "Denizens! You fight a war that could have been prevented. Your leader withholds information from you, information that could have saved countless lives."

"Kill the beast!" The charcoal skinned Troll shouted. A few reluctant Trolls threw their spears at The Gazer. The spears passed through the Dragon's scales, without leaving a scratch, and were disintegrated before they passed to the other side.

"Trygon! Your ancestors would be ashamed if they saw what you have become. You have embraced hell's corruption! Your skin has been charred by its fires, and tusks have grown from your visage in the image of Demons. You have become a hell spawn. Your people follow a monster, not a Troll!"

"Silence! After centuries of exile, my people will taste victory! They will return to their ancestral lands!"

"Your people have been invited back to the northern lands, and you have denied them a peaceful return! You fight for blood to satisfy your enslavers. The price of hell's service is death, and you must fulfill it. That is what you have become; a servant to hell."

"Denizens! Do not be swayed by his deceit! He tricks you! He tells lies to weaken your resolve with the hope of exiling you to the marshes once more! Slay the northern scum and reclaim what's rightfully yours!"

The battle started once again. "Then so it shall be." The light changed to a dark red.

***

The Observatory was filled with a white light, and it forced Violet to cover her eyes.

"The Gazer has joined the battle." Diana murmured.

"That's him? I can't even see anything!" She said, still covering her eyes.

"Look now, the light is softening."

Violet looked into the pool, the light was now blue, and it emanated from a serpent shape. "Wow..." Violet was wonderstruck. "He's so bright... It's breathtaking."

"Today you will see why he is the strongest being of our world. Few people have ever seen The Gazer fight, let alone fight against him. During your time here you have become part of some very exclusive groups, my girl."

***

In the hospital room, Lindbel was shining a flashlight into Violet's eyes. There were some signs of reaction. This was good, her senses were starting to function once more.

***

The Astral Dragon's touch was fatal. He was moving across the battlefield through the southern army, swatting at his enemies with his tail, but it did not hit them; it passed through them. It would set them ablaze into blue and white star fire, becoming dust in a matter of moments. All projectiles that were shot at him passed through his ethereal body, and left nothing but dust on the ground. The Gazer had put a dent into the southern forces, but many still remained. The Denizens were split; some were caught between The Gazer and the northern army, while others were cut off from the battle, not so eager to join the fight against their new foe.

The Denizens that were caught between the northern army and The Gazer were beginning to lose moral. Some of them pleaded for mercy, surrendering to the northern forces, while others simply deserted their allies.

Kenghala had fallen to the northern army. He had been speared through the back by one of the Sea Folks icicles, pinning him to the ground. After that, he was impaled by Elven spears. When he had finally been slain, countless souls escaped his body towards the sky, cries of joy coming from all of them.

Trygon left the frontline to face The Gazer. "Beast!" He shouted, and The Gazer turned towards him. "You will die today!"

"Yes, show your people what you really are, demon!" The Gazer called across the battlefield. All eyes were watching the encounter, the battle paused again.

"I know your tricks! If we need magic, then we'll have magic!" The Troll started sprinting towards The Gazer, flames beginning to envelop him. He jumped towards The Gazer, still very far away, and an explosion came from his body, sending ash into the sky and flames outwards across the battlefield, scorching the terrain and singing the leaves of the forest. From the explosion came a fiery being with horns jutting from its skull. It sailed through the air, arms extended, and collided with The Gazer.

A ring of fire formed around the two combatants. Blue and red streaks ran through its perimeter. The demon wrestled to get hold of The

Gazer's body, but the serpent slid through its grasp time and time again. The Gazer wrapped itself around the Demon, constricting it. "Trygon, the powers of hell hold a steep price. You have damned yourself to a fate worse than death."

"You have betrayed your world, Dragon! You were meant to be a peacekeeper between the nations of our world, but you stood by for centuries as my people suffered in the swamps. You have favored the northern races since the beginning of time!" A violent explosion came from the Demon, freeing itself from The Gazer's hold. They were separated by an expanse of blazing earth.

"I have done my duty!" The Gazer shouted, white fire starting to gather in its transparent body. "Your people have put races into extinction! You complain to me how you were mistreated while you have the blood of millions on your hands!"

A sword of blazing dark fire formed in Trygon's hand. He charged the Dragon once more, and The Gazer put his whole body into a swing with his tail, colliding with Trygon and sending the Demon to the edge of the circle, engulfed in blue flames. The sword fell to the ground, vanishing as it touched the burning battlefield, sending an ebon flare upwards. The enveloping fire dissipated, leaving only a thick boned skeleton with horns laying against the perimeter of the ring. The bones began to darken as they stood up from the ground, and exploded into black flames. The circle shot black flames into the sky, blotting out the sun. The sky was pitch black, leaving the field to be lit only by the Phoenix above the northern army and The Gazer's body still shining a white light across the entire battlefield.

"You are no protector." The Demon said, slowly approaching the dragon. "You condemned my people to a fate they did not deserve. Today, they will return home, victorious!" A black spear manifested in the Demons hand, its black flames mingled with searing white fire.

The spear was thrown through the air, sailing into one of The Gazer's stars and tainting it black. A cry of pain came from the serpent as it fell to the ground. The Demon laid its foot upon the Dragon's chest, forming another black spear in his hand. "A new defender will now watch over this world, and a different people will rise to greatness." He rose the spear above his head, holding it with both hands.

The Gazer's maw opened, letting loose a cascade of white star fire upon the Demon's body. The Demon faltered, dropping the spear and stepping back with its arms in front of its face. Trygon's screams resonated across the battlefield. The Gazer pursued the Demon, forcing him back against the wall of the circle and down onto the ground. When the fire finally abated, one of The Gazer's stars extinguished as well, leaving his lower half completely transparent. The darkness cleared from the sky, returning the sun to illuminate the scorched earth. Where the star fire had bleached the ground, a green Troll now lay in the white dirt. It did not have tusks, and its eyes were brown, not red.

"How long has it been Trygon? How long since you were in your own body?" The Gazer asked. The white light from his body changed to purple.

Sobs could be heard from the dirt.

"Why did you accept the Demons' strength? You knew that it would only bring suffering."

The Troll lifted his head from the bleached soil. "I was convinced it was the only way to deliver what my people wanted. We could have never overpowered the northern races with what we had. Our exile caused a great agony among the southern races, they needed to return home to the north."

A long pause passed between them. "Trygon, you have committed crimes against the entirety of the Dreamscape, I am sorry, but you cannot go unpunished." The Gazer said.

The Troll was a husk. Not only had he failed his people, he had failed his ancestors; his world as a whole.

Chapter Thirty One
Witness to Victory

Diana and Violet were in the Observatory. The war had ended in Trygon's defeat, and Violet could barely contain her excitement. She would be going home!

"That battle seems to have taken much out of The Gazer. Two of his stars have extinguished and another has been tainted."

"What does that mean though? He can still send me home, right?" Violet didn't want to wait any longer, the sooner she could return home the better.

"The stars of his body symbolize his energy. When he was above the battlefield he had eight in his body, but he lost one immediately after he landed into the battle, another when he purified Trygon, and the third was tainted by the Demon's black fire. Five now remain, with luck, he may still return you home, my dear."

"That's great!" Violet gave Diana a hug, squeezing a bit too hard due to her excitement. "Thank you so much for everything you've done for me." She whispered to Diana.

"I would have it no other way, Violet."

A call came down the stairs. "My Queen! A message has arrived from the battlefield. The trees claim that the war has been won! They ask of anyone who is capable that they come to the battlefield as soon as possible."

"Thank you, we will be up in a moment!" She answered.

Diana turned back to Violet. "You should stay here until we return. I would hate to keep you any longer than you must, but perhaps such a gruesome scene would be better unseen."

Violet wanted to go very badly, but she knew that Diana was right. "When will you return?"

"We will depart for the Lake of Lenidral as soon as possible. It is a two day journey there, and two days back. We will return in four days' time. Again, I am sorry that you have to wait longer still, but it will soon be over."

Diana led a group of people to the lake that afternoon, and Violet watched from her bedroom window as they faded from view.

Chapter Thirty Two
The Aftermath

The war was over, but its end only signified the beginning of great toils. Neither army celebrated. The northern races had lost many people, and the southern had lost even more. Not one of them had gone without losing a friend in the past three days. The bodies were laid out across the battlefield in lines. Dwarves beside Goblins, Elves beside Trolls; their race did not matter anymore. Word was sent to Heidskun of the war's end, and within the week mourners came to say their farewells.

The bodies were too great in numbers to be brought home, so a funeral would be held in the battlefield; a mass cremation of fallen warriors.

A prayer was said for everyone in a whole, and then each race said a prayer for their own people.

The smell of burning flesh filled the air for miles. Ashes were blown by a wind into the north sky, scattering across the forests as far as the eye could see.

"May you all learn from this war," The Gazer was telling all who remained after the funeral, "Do not repeat the actions of the past. Forgive one another for each other's transgressions. A war of this gravity must never again come to pass in the history of our world. Let it be known, from this day forth the southern races and the northern races have reunited under one banner. They shall no longer be known as either southern or northern, they will be known as The Dreamscape Coalition."

A cheer arose from all of the remaining attendants.

"All of you may return to the land that you call home, whether that be your home from centuries long ago, or your home from recent years."

All of the races made their way to the north, leaving their weapons on the battlefield.

The Gazer stayed; only he, Trygon and Hestaphal still remained. "Trygon," The Gazer turned to the Troll, "you must now answer for your crimes against the Dreamscape. What defense do you offer?"

The green skinned Troll still sat in the bleached dirt. "I offer no defense, I made what I believed to be the right choice, and I have been proven wrong. My punishment has been justified." The Troll now laid prostrate on the ground before The Gazer.

"Trygon, by my right as defender of this world, I hereby declare you as being forsaken. On this battlefield you will die, and here you will stay for eternity. You will be a reminder to those who would cause harm to the world as you now have; this will be the fate that awaits them."

A gallows was brought out onto the battlefield, and upon it Trygon waited. His head was put into the noose, and the floor opened beneath him.

"You have made the change that you sought to effect, but at what cost?" The living left the field.

Only the hanging body of a Troll now remained on the battlefield, among a field of ash and char.

Chapter Thirty Three
Resettlement

All of the races returned to their homes from centuries ago. The Goblins returned to the mountain range, to their old caverns in the mountainsides. It had been so long since they lived in their dark abodes that their sight was no longer adjusted to its shadows. But they were determined to live in their caves once more.

***

The cavern Fairies illuminated the caves with their faint luminescence. Despite how dimly they glowed, it was enough light for the Goblins to see. They built huts in the dark with walls of stone and dead branches and rooves of dry grass. They established farms in the dampest reaches of the caves, harvesting edible fungus and farming slugs for their food. They were contented with their lives once more. They had so badly missed the caves; the swamps were muddy, wet and cold, the light hurt their eyes for a very long time, but they had eventually adjusted. Now, within weeks, they were readjusted to the dark.

***

The Trolls went two different ways. The cave Trolls returned to their shallow caves at the foot of the mountains. The caves were their homes, but they lived beyond its walls. They would hunt wildlife for food and forage for sustenance in the surrounding forests. The jungle Trolls returned to their densely vegetated forests to the northwest. Trees that stood half the height of the mother tree covered the land in their homeland. They rebuilt their homes in the canopies of their chosen tree. They connected their homes to one another with bridges that hung high above the ground. They hunted in the jungle below and fished at the nearby coast. They hung lines across the base of the bridges to hang meat from. Both Troll communities lived primitive lives, but the jungle Trolls lived together, working together, while the cave Trolls lived alone, rarely ever seeing one another.

***

The Ogres returned to the foothills near the Centaurs' meadows. They lived in small communities, working together to herd large animals into pens and gather what food they could from the forest. They built crude stone hovels with straw rooves. The structures did not have windows, and the doorways were just a section that they would not place any stone. They lived a simple life, but it was the life that the Ogres had missed for so long. And now, finally, they had that life back.

***

The Cyclopes returned to the highest peaks of the mountain range, leaving their homes only on the rare occasion that they had to find more food. The Cyclopes would bring a lot of food back into the mountains with them so that they rarely had to leave their frigid peaks. They lived in isolation; they claimed territory and stayed out of each other's land. They carried whole buffaloes into their lairs, hanging them for later. Sometimes, they would be fortunate enough to find mountain goats, and could capture them for later as well. The Cyclopes no longer had to share, and they were happy.

***

The Minotaurs returned to the valleys to the far north. The crevices they called home were barren wastelands. To the Minotaurs, however, they were sanctuaries. They could brawl without being interrupted by others, and they didn't have to worry about damaging the forest and incurring the wrath of nature. They could grind their horns against the stone walls of the chasms and the higher points in the valleys were hospitable for them. The valley floors were covered in grass and small lakes could be found around the winding maze of crevices. The Minotaurs were overjoyed to have their rift back after so long of being in marshlands.

***

At the Dwarf kingdom, Aldreit was officially coronated. Gein had fallen during the war, and Breitol had nearly drowned after being swept into the lake by the Hydra. Aldreit now sat in his throne, looking at the world differently. He had to govern this mountain?

"Breitol, I think that our father has made a mistake."

Breitol turned to Aldreit. "A mistake about what?"

"I shouldn't be king. I could never govern these Dwarves; the people I have known as friends all my life. How could I decide what they do in their lives?"

"Brother, these Dwarves know you well, which gives them all the more reason to want to follow you into the most hopeless of wars. Our father has made no mistake, you will find your way, brother. Give it time."

***

The Elf king was sitting in his throne, speaking with his advisor. "Well, Sikator, it appears you were mistaken."

"About what, my lord?"

"About the war, of course. It appears that the Dreamscape Coalition have become a single people. The war has not torn us apart, it has brought us together."

"In this case, my lord, I am glad that I was wrong."

***

Life for the Sea Folk became rather boring once more. They had nothing more to do now than before the war. They swam around in the deep sea simply maintaining their society.

Silvayna and Pricus had begun to talk. They wanted to bring their two peoples together, in hopes of bringing more enjoyment to their lives. The Capricorns grew bored quickly, so perhaps the Sea Folk could entertain them by teaching them new things. And the Sea Folk generally didn't play games; "they need to lighten up," Silvayna thought.

They could also learn from each other. The Sea Folk were adept in frost magic, while the Capricorns enjoyed aquamancy; perhaps they could teach each other how to use certain spells.

Silvayna secretly enjoyed talking to Pricus, and Pricus enjoyed the change of company. Even if they accomplished very little with their discussions, maybe having to keep meeting wasn't such a bad thing?

***

The Centaurs did not enjoy having such close company at first, especially not the Ogres, but they eventually grew acquainted, and the Centaurs began to herd animals as well. They did not use the animals for meat as the Ogres did however; they used them for what they could give. They herded cows for milk, and sheep for their wool. There were indeed benefits to having their new neighbors.

***

The Dryads watched over the trees, making sure that the southern races wouldn't harm the trees. They were glad to see that the Goblins only took dead branches from the forest floor instead of tearing live branches from the surrounding trees. They eventually became lax with their guarding, at ease with how the new inhabitants treated the forests and jungles with respect.

***

The Shapeshifters ran surveillance over the southern races for a short while after the war, but soon deemed them safe. They hid as birds in trees, or as rats in holes to keep an eye on the returning races. They were hopeful, but security was necessary; they could never be too sure.

***

A trade center was established by the Gnomes in between the domains of the new Dreamscape Coalition. The different races could bring trade goods to exchange for various items they might need. The Gnomes sold various machines that helped with the races' daily lives, and, because of this trade center, bonds were formed between races and made stronger. In the end, the races were working together on various matters. The races had forgiven each other for the war, and it had quickly been swept into the sands of time.

***

The only people who weren't especially happy were the Fairies. The cave Fairies didn't mind living with the Goblins; they kind of enjoyed being helpful for them, because the Goblins helped them in return.

The other Fairies, however, were a bit more reluctant to accept their new neighbors.

"Did you see the Ogres? They are so ugly!"

"I know! And the Minotaurs, with their ugly cow faces." The Fairy motioned as though she would vomit.

The Fairies were a shallow group. They judged the worth of someone by their attractiveness. To them, the worst crime you could commit was being unpleasant to the eye. They were most certainly unhappy with the outcome of this war.

Chapter Thirty Four
Remorse

Hestaphal was reluctant to return to Heidskun. He knew Violet would be there and he did not want to face her yet again. Perhaps, if he was lucky, she would not be as upset with him. Time had passed since he had last spoken to her, and maybe she had forgiven him. When he arrived at the mother tree, Diana was at the base of the tree. She had just come from one of the doors when she saw Hestaphal in the doorway to the outside.

She walked over to him, pushing him back out of the door. "You want to talk to her, don't you?"

Hestaphal sighed, "I don't really want to, but I have to apologize at least one more time before she leaves. Do you think she will forgive me this time, now that it's over?

"I somehow doubt it. Violet is right to be upset with you though, you imprisoned her and denied her the right to return home."

"I fully accept that I have done her wrong, but I had no better option."

"There is always another option."

"When I look back at it now, yes, there were many possible options. But at the time when the decision was made, and when I didn't know better, I made the decision that appeared to be the best with the information I had. I cannot change what happened, and I would not if I could."

"Well, I'm sure she will be glad to hear that you don't regret keeping her against her will, Hestaphal." Diana entered the tree once more. "She's in her room; you know where it is." Diana disappeared behind one of the ground floor doors.

Hestaphal started up the stairs to Violet's room. He did not want to do this again, but he would forever be upset with himself if he let her leave without clearing his conscience.

When he arrived at her door, he heard laughter from the other side. He knocked.

"Come in."

Hestaphal pulled aside the curtain, seeing Violet and Taivna sitting on the bed, talking. Violet's expression quickly changed from being happy to dismal. "What do you want?" She asked, clearly not caring about what he wanted.

Hestaphal entered the room, the curtain falling into place behind him. "I want to apologize once more for what I did to you."

"Why? Are you still unhappy with yourself?" Violet scoffed.

"How very gracious of you. Yes, I detest my own actions, but I did it for what I thought would be a validating reason. I was mistaken, and for that, I am sorry."

"Well I thought we had already gone over this and it was settled?"

"We both know that you did not forgive me. I would like to make it up to you, however that may be."

"First off, you could stop talking about it."

"It would be my pleasure."

"And secondly, you could leave, maybe."

"And if I did, you would forgive me?"

"It's a start."

"That's not good enough. I need to know that you will honestly forgive me and you won't harbor resentment over it."

"Well, I'm sorry to tell you, but most people don't really appreciate wrongful imprisonment." Violet crossed her arms.

This was going nowhere. "Violet, you need to understand, you have indirectly saved thousands of lives and amended millennium old hatreds. You have done this world a great deed at such a small cost. The leaders of this world will remember you for centuries, long after you have left. Is that not compensation for your lost time?"

"Maybe if I had been given a choice I would have made the right one. I have a moral compass, you know? Now, will you leave?"

"Do you forgive me?"

"What does it matter if I do?"

"To me, it means my sanity."

"Then go insane. But do it outside please."

Hestaphal waited. He could not believe this girl could be so bull headed. "Very well. May your years bring you the wisdom to see your errors, Violet Glendale, and may my own grant me a free conscience." And he left.

***

After Hestaphal left, neither Violet nor Taivna said anything for a short while. Violet started the conversation once more.

"Sorry." She said.

"For what?" The Elf boy asked.

"That you had to see that."

"I'm not the one you should apologize to. He wants to make amends with you. Why won't you forgive him?"

Violet stood up from the bed. "Are you defending him?" She accused.

"If that's how you want to see it, then yes. But surely you understand that what he did was the right thing to do, do you not?"

"That's not the point. The point is he denied me my freedom. I was forced to stay here against my will."

"Did you not enjoy being here? Did we not make it comfortable enough for you? Or were you just bored of us?"

"No... That's not what I meant."

"Well that's how it sounds." Taivna walked to the doorway. "Maybe you'll come to your senses before you leave. In case I don't see you again, I hope you like being home again."

And he left. Once more, Violet was left with her regret. "How do I always manage to screw everything up?" She thought to herself.

***

Hestaphal had gone back downstairs to find Diana. He checked the room she had gone in when he left, and he found that she was still there. She was sitting behind a desk against the far wall with a picture in her hands.

She looked up when Hestaphal came in, and hid the picture in a desk drawer. "Hello, Hestaphal." She sounded as if she had been crying. "Did it go well with Violet?"

Hestaphal closed the door. "No. She refuses to forgive me. Are you okay?"

"Yes, of course. Was she upset with you still?"

"Yes, very much so. What was that you were holding?"

"What do you mean?"

"You were holding something when I came in and put it away. What was it?"

"Oh, nothing. Have you heard from The Gazer yet?"

"No, I haven't. Diana, what's wrong?"

"Nothing, nothing's wrong. I just hope she gets home safely."

"Diana, you aren't hiding it very well. You're upset that she is leaving, aren't you?"

"Of course not. The girl doesn't want to be here, so there's no reason for me to keep her any longer than she has to stay. Wouldn't you agree?"

"Don't redirect this to me. It was a picture wasn't it? The thing you were holding?"

Tears were starting to gather at the edge of her eyes. She refused to answer.

Hestaphal walked to the desk, opening one of the drawers and removing the picture. Inside the frame was a photograph of Diana and a young girl that looked strikingly similar to Violet. "Who is this?"

Diana snatched the photo out of his hand, holding it against her chest. "It doesn't matter to you."

"She looks like Glendale."

Diana shuddered. Tears began to stream down her cheeks as she struggled to hold back sobs.

Hestaphal looked at Diana. "The girl also looks like you in some ways. Did you have a daughter?"

"Leave me be, Hestaphal." Diana sat back in the chair, looking down at the picture in her lap.

"Violet reminds her of you, doesn't she? That's why you're so fond of her. Where is your daughter?"

Diana only shook her head.

"I-. I'm sorry. What was her name?"

Between breaths Diana murmured "Celia."

"I did not know you had a daughter."

Diana was taking deep breaths to calm herself. "Very few people ever knew. She was born in secret, but I had the Gnomes take a photo of us to keep as a memory. This room is off limits to everyone else, because it's the only place in our world that has any evidence of her existence."

"What happened to her?"

Diana shivered once more. "I don't know. She went on a voyage across seas and she never returned."

"I see. How long has she been gone?"

"She left nearly two centuries ago. Long before I ever knew you."

Hestaphal knelt beside Diana. "And now you've reopened this wound. Make the most of your time with the girl, because it will only hurt once she has gone."

"Leave me be, Hestaphal."

Hestaphal walked to the door and set his hand on the knob.

"Hestaphal?"

"What is it, Diana?"

"Please, do not tell anyone of this. Of my daughter."

"Not a soul."

"Thank you." She said through a pained smile.

And he left.

***

Violet had to make things right. She didn't want to forgive Hestaphal, but, until she did, Taivna would not speak to her. She started down the stairs to find Hestaphal, seeing him at the base of the tree having just left a room in the corner.

He was walking towards the exit. She didn't want to shout down at him, so she just sped up. She had to play this right, she couldn't seem eager, but she couldn't seem reluctant. She needed to be genuine.

She was taking the steps two at a time going at a breakneck pace. When she finally got to the base of the tree she shoved the door to the outside open. The door smacked against the tree, making a loud noise. Hestaphal was standing in the courtyard talking to an Elf, but now they were both looking at her in the doorway.

Already, Violet looked distressed. This was not the start she had planned for. "Hestaphal," she called over while running a hand through her hair, trying to look casual despite her appearance, "can I talk to you?"

Hestaphal said goodbye to the Elf, who walked to the courtyard behind the tree. Hestaphal walked over to Violet. "What is it now? Would you like to argue with me more?"

"Uh, no. Actually, I came to apologize. I'm, um, I'm not very good with apologies, so hear me out. I'm sorry for not forgiving you, ugh no that sounds arrogant. I'm sorry for being rude to you. I should have accepted your apology instead of denying you a clear conscience. I forgive you for what you had to do, and I understand if you don't think I deserve to be forgiven now."

Hestaphal paused before answering. "Thank you for forgiving me. I accept your apology, Violet Glendale. I'd say you handled that apology pretty well."

"Thanks." Violet lowered her head a bit. "I, um. I should go now."

"Farewell, Violet. Have a safe return home."

~ 122 ~

"Thanks, you too."

***

Now Violet had to find Taivna. She hadn't seen which way he went on the stairs. Perhaps he had started cleaning rooms again. But which did he start again with?

Violet didn't like the idea of peeking into peoples' rooms, but if she had to do that to find Taivna, then she might just stoop to that level. She asked one of the Elf housekeepers if they had seen him, and they told her that Taivna should be near the upper rooms. She thanked them and started up the stairs.

She saw him higher up the stairs, nearly three rings up and around the tree. She started going a bit faster up the stairs, glad that she never felt tired in this world. He went into a room higher up, and Violet tried to hurry, hoping to meet him in that room instead of on the stairs.

She gets to the room and goes to open the curtain, but he opens it first. Instead of touching the curtain, her hand paws his face, causing him to flinch back. "Oh! Sorry! I was tr-"

"I know what you were doing. What is it?"

"Well, I wanted to let you know I fixed things with Hestaphal."

"That was quick. Does my opinion matter that much to you?"

Violet blushed a bit, turning her face away. "No, of course not! I just thought it was the right thing to do."

"Well, I'm glad you fixed your moral compass, it seemed to be a bit askew for a while. Okay, well I'm sorry to have to end this talk, but I need to get back to work. I'll come find you later, okay?"

"O-Okay. See you." Violet moved aside for Taivna to pass. How come being nice never had immediate results? Or at least, never the results she wanted.

Chapter Thirty Five

Reclusion

The Gazer returned to his temple, his energy was depleting. He had underestimated the Demon's grip on Trygon, and the power that it contained. His tail had faded, completely transparent from the loss of three stars. Two of them would return in time, but he had never had a star turn black. There was no guarantee for the third one.

He made his way to the back of the temple, the walls became brighter and more reflective the further back he went. He reached the end of the hall and entered into the back room. All surfaces were mirrors, the illusion of infinity only broken by the doorway. The room lit up as white, and transitioned into purple with his body.

The Gazer laid down in the center of the room. The mortal eye would be blinded by the light, but he was accustomed to it. He was tired; the battle had drained him of his energy, he had used nearly half of his stars as fuel during the war, and now he had to recuperate. Soon, he could send the girl home, but for now he had to rest.

***

At Heidskun, Violet was sick of being in the Dreamscape. She was drawing her house once more, finishing touches here and there. She thought it looked accurate to her memory of it.

Violet had noticed the rock starting to shrink. It was gradual, but it had visibly shrunk since Taivna had given it to her. Right now she was drawing the grass on her lawn. She had done a rough work of it before, but now she had decided to detail it more.

Violet stood up to stretch her body out a bit. She raised her arms over her head and reached for the ceiling while standing on the tips of her toes. While she was stretching, Diana came into the room.

"Hello, Violet."

Violet recoiled a bit, but managed to keep her balance. She had thought she would be alone for a while. "Uh, hi Diana. Why can't you knock when you come in?"

"Oh, I'm sorry. I just wanted to come talk to you for a little bit."

"Yeah, no, sorry. It's fine. What did you want to talk about?"

"I just thought I would come see how you were doing. Why don't we go sit down?" She asked while gesturing towards the bedroom.

They went and sat on the bed. After a short time of silence, Diana starts the conversation again.

"So. I bet you're excited to be going home, right?"

"Yeah, kind of."

"Only a little? Not even a week ago you couldn't wait to get back. So what's happened since then?"

"Nothing, I guess."

"If you don't know, how is anyone supposed to help you?"

"Well, I guess there is something, but it's silly. I shouldn't care about that boy anyways. It's not like I even really know him, and besides, I won't know him for much longer."

Another brief pause.

"You know, I had a daughter once, a long time ago. She had long blond hair and she was about your age, in relativity to our life expectancies, when I last saw her." She laughed once. "It's kind of nice actually, you remind me a lot of her. Maybe she is still out there somewhere." Diana propped her arms against her knees and laid her head in her hands.

Violet didn't really know what to say.

"Sorry if that made you uncomfortable; I was just thinking out loud again."

"No, that's fine. Um, if you don't mind me asking, what happened to her?"

"My daughter? She decided that she wanted to see what lay on the other side of the sea. So she left one day with a crew, promising me that she would come visit me sometime. I haven't seen her since. I spend most of my time in the Observatory looking for her. Even just to know that she's okay would make a world of difference." She let a sharp exhale escape from her nose. "It's kind of silly isn't it? You give birth to a child and from the moment you meet them, you're willing to do anything to keep them safe. You don't even know them and they mean more to you than anything else." Diana sat straight again. "But I guess you wouldn't really know that feeling yet." She wrapped an arm around Violet's shoulders pulling her closer. "Promise me something, will you? Promise me that when you have a child you will take care of them. That you will give them the best life that you can and you'll always keep them safe. Don't let them do anything dangerous unless they know all the possible threats, and always have a spot in your heart for them, no matter how badly they hurt you. Can you promise me that?"

"I'll try my best to keep that promise."

Diana gave Violet a hug, whispering into her ear. "Thank you. I know it's a lot to ask, but I somehow know that you will do just fine."

They let each other go, and Diana wiped her eyes. "I guess I should go make sure everything is running smoothly." Diana said, getting up from the bed. She walked to the doorway and Violet felt that she should say something. But what?

Diana left the room, and Violet wished she could have thought of something.

***

The hospital room was quiet. Diana sat in her chair still beside Violet. She had finished her latest book two days ago and Bryan had yet to bring her another. It had been nearly a week since Lindbel had noticed Violet's pupils reacting to the flashlight, and nothing new had come up since then, but Diana still carried hope from that day. Bryan and Peter were going to visit tonight after Bryan was finished work, and Diana was excited to see them again. Their visits were her greatest support.

***

The room had changed from purple to blue when a knock was heard from outside. Very few people had ever tread this far into The Gazer's temple. When they did, they either had a serious concern, or a death wish.

The Astral Dragon unfurled in the center of the room. "Which one are you," The Gazer called, "the death wish or the concern?"

"Someone who you owe." A voice called back.

"Shapeshifter, I will return the girl when I am able to." He said back, coiling tightly in the center of the room once more.

"What do you mean? Are you not able to right now?"

"Your war has drained me of energy. I must wait for my stars to reignite. I assure you, the girl will be sent home when I can fulfill her request. It takes more energy than I currently have to shatter the barrier of rest."

Hestaphal still had more questions. "What do you mean 'shatter the barrier'? How long until you can send her home?"

"The barrier of rest is what keeps someone asleep. If I am to wake

~ 126 ~

her up in her own world, then I will need my full potential."

"Do you mean to tell me that she is asleep?"

"I knew you could figure it out. Now, go reason it out on your own; I must rest if you want me to send her back."

"Not so fast, I only have more questions than when I first came to you. If she is asleep, then does that mean we are in her dream? What happens to us if she wakes up?"

The Gazer let out a long sigh while he uncurled once more. "Shapeshifter, she is asleep in her own world. Dreams do not work the way you think they do. When you dream at night you visit another world that's as real as your own; it just belongs to a different reality than your own. She has been here for so long because she is in a coma. Do you not remember her? It is not the first time she has come here. Every night when she dreams, she is here. You have never seen her, because she wakes up in her own world and is torn out of our own world. I have seen her countless times in our world, but, this time, she did not leave when she usually would have, which is what caught my attention."

"So, if she wakes up? Then what?"

"Then nothing. Our world will continue as usual, except she will have returned home. She will return every night that she dreams for as long as she lives."

Hestaphal took a moment to gather his thoughts. "Why should I believe you? How would you know anything about this?"

"What am I to this world?"

"The Warden, you keep peace in our world."

"Not only this world. I am one of many Wardens. I monitor this world and many others, maintaining stability and fixing irregularities. This girl is welcome in our world for only so long. She has been here longer than she should be and is starting to cause abnormalities. She has forged relationship with our world's people that will not fade quickly and will change their futures. She has caused irreversible change, this is why she must go. She may return at later points in time, but this session has gone on for too long."

"When she is in our world, is she as real as we are?"

"Yes, which is the same when you dream. When you visit the other realities you are bound to both your reality and this new reality you have found. Death is transferable."

"So, if I died in my dream, I would die in my own world?"

"I told you that you could reason it out. But rarely ever does someone die in their dreams. All races of all realities have the ability to end their connection to these new realities at any given moment. They wake themselves up, or are woken up, and the threat no longer exists."

"Then how can someone die in their dreams if they can end them before they die?

"You're circling back now. Forced rest, we talked about this. The girl is in a coma, she cannot wake herself up. When someone falls into a coma, they are stuck in their other world and it is up to a Warden to return them home. So if she were to die before I could return her home, then she could do nothing about it; she would expire in her own world too."

This was a lot of information for Hestaphal.

"How many days until you can return her home?" He asked.

"I will need six days' rest; two for each extinguished star to reignite. It has been four days since the end of the war, so only two still remain. However, the tainted star may be a different case; for all I know it may never return. It takes the power of six stars to shatter the barrier and return her home. Since I will only have one star after the ritual, I will be very weak for the following twelve days. The stars do not return one at a time, they reignite all together, so I will have but one star for the duration."

"Then I will leave you to rest. The sooner the girl is free of danger the sooner I can have peace of mind."

"Bring her to my temple in two days. I will not be able to return to my temple on my own when I am so weak, so it is best that the ritual is done here, where I rest."

"Very well. Farewell, Gazer."

"Keep her safe, Shapeshifter."

Chapter Thirty Six
Return

Violet was waiting in her room. Hestaphal had told her a couple days ago that she would be going home today, and now the day was here. The sun was bright in the sky and the clouds were sparse. Violet had hardly slept that night, but it made no difference since she never felt tired in the Dreamscape. Her excitement had stopped here from passing the night away swiftly, she had had to wait until the morning when the others were awake as well.

Violet had decided to finish the drawing of her home overnight instead of laying on the bed for hours. The drawing was accurate to the very last detail. She had drawn small ridges on the blades of grass and drawn the lines on the siding of her home. It had been difficult to learn the heat to color ratio, but eventually she had been able to find the right color on the first try every time, fifty percent of the time. At least, that's how she had described it to Taivna.

Hestaphal had explained his conversation with The Gazer to Violet, who had understood even less than he had when The Gazer told him. However, eventually she had caught on. It eased her mind that she would be able to visit them at night, that she wouldn't just be abandoning them.

At least, that's how she felt about it; that she was abandoning them.

Violet had asked Hestaphal if she could be there when he explained this all to Diana, and he had agreed. He told her that they would tell her today, on the day that she was to leave. It would help to ease her pain, he thought.

A knock came at Violet's doorway.

"Come in" She called.

Hestaphal pulled aside the curtain and stepped into the room. "Are you ready to go home?" He asked Violet.

Violet sat up from the bed, wearing her own clothes once more. "I've been ready for weeks." She said, stretching her arms out over her head.

"Perfect. Then let's go see Diana before we leave. No doubt she would like to say farewell, and we still have to tell her you'll be back." He said with a wink.

The pair started up the stairs towards the canopy of the tree. The stairs seemed much longer than usual to Violet, as if the tree had grown. But that was unlikely.

They arrived at Diana's doorway, and Hestaphal waited before knocking. They could hear crying on the other side. They exchanged a glance but said nothing. Hestaphal knocked.

"One second, please." Diana answered, her voice was fragile. Footsteps sounded across the floor into the washroom. A few moments later the footsteps returned and the curtain opened, revealing a woman with red rings around her eyes and slightly damp cheeks. "Hello, you two. Would you like to come in?" She asked, bringing the curtain aside with herself. She had regained her composure before opening the curtain.

The two found a seat in the room and waited. Diana sat upon the stool in front of her mirror once more, Violet was sat on the bed and Hestaphal was leaning on the window sill, the breeze playing with his silver sleeves.

Diana began again. "So you two will be leaving soon for the temple, right?"

"Yes," Hestaphal answered. "We thought it would be best if we came and said goodbye first."

"That's very considerate of you both." She said, wiping below her eyes once more.

"But there is one other thing we wanted to share with you." Diana's eyes narrowed, looking back and forth between the two. "When I spoke with The Gazer, he explained something to me. Our world is now connected to Violet permanently. But that's not all. Violet is asleep in her own world right now; she is in a coma." This earned a worried look from Diana. "Whenever Violet dreams she ends up in our world."

"So... You mean that... She'll be coming back?"

"Yes, Diana. This isn't goodbye forever, you will see each other most days, whenever Violet dreams at night."

Diana started to tear up again, but now it was from joy. Words escaped her. Violet got up from the bed and walked over to her. She gave Diana a hug, "This means I can keep you up to speed on our promise" She whispered to her.

Diana laughed with relief. "Even if you couldn't, I still had faith in you keeping it." They let go of each other.

Hestaphal walked towards the doorway. "So, I think it's about time I let you get home, don't you think?"

"Good bye, Violet." Diana said, placing a hand on Violet's shoulder. "Go and wake your family up from their nightmare."

They hugged once more, and Violet followed Hestaphal out of the room and down the stairs.

"Do you want to say goodbye to your boy?" Hestaphal asked over his shoulder.

"He's not 'my boy', he's just a friend."

"Sure seems like it." Hestaphal teased. "So, is that a yes?"

Violet rolled her eyes. "You keep going to the courtyard, it will only make it awkward with you watching over my shoulder."

"Have it your way; I'll be waiting outside."

Violet asked one of the other housekeepers for directions. They told her that he was supposed to be bringing towels to her room any minute. She thanked them and started running down the stairs to her room.

When she got to her room, she checked to see if he was there. She was in luck; he hadn't arrived yet. Violet wanted to catch his attention the moment he walked in, but she wasn't sure how. She sat on the bed, trying to think of a way. A raven landed outside her window, she noticed it but thought nothing of it. As long as her window was shut, she didn't mind.

She laid back on the bed, her head against the backboard, and arched her legs. Her skirt fell back against her, fully revealing her legs. She tucked the skirt between her legs. She thought about what she looked like from the front, thinking of how someone could see under her skirt. "That's a bit too much." She thought to herself. She sat at the edge of the bed once more, thinking of what to do. She tried laying on her stomach facing the door. "This might work" she thought. After a couple minutes of waiting, her neck got sore though, and she had to lay her head down on the bed. She ended up changing position again. This time she tried laying backwards on the bed, her legs climbing up above the headboard. Her skirt fell down against her once more and she tucked it between her legs. The headboard was cold against the bottoms of her legs, and she didn't really have a good view of the door. How could she know what he thought if she couldn't see his face? She swung her legs around the edge of the bed again. She threw around a few other ideas, maybe she could be in the bath to try and be able to tease him about that again, or maybe she could just hug one of the bed poles. "Diana was right," She thought, "Love makes you silly." Why should she sit all these ways? She doesn't have to impress him, if he needs to be impressed then it's not right. "Oh, what am I talking about? I'm in a dream, it doesn't matter in the first place."

When he finally came into the room, Violet was sitting normally on the edge of the bed, her hands between her legs in the creases of her skirt. He was carrying towels. "Oh, hi Violet. Aren't you going home today?"

Violet's mouth dropped a bit. "Really? That's the first thing you ask me? I stay to say goodbye to you, and to talk to you, and you ask me when I'm leaving? What's wrong with you?"

"I'm sorry, I just didn't think that you would still be here, I thought you had left early this morning. I'm glad that you came to say goodbye and all, I just didn't expect to get to see you again. I'm surprised."

Violet took the towels from him, setting them on the bed, and slapped his head to one side. She hugged him and put her head on his other shoulder.

"So…" He started.

She hushed him.

They stayed that way for a short while.

"Are you mad at me or happy to see me? Because there are a lot of mixed signals here."

"Can't I be both?" She pushed him away playfully.

"I-. I guess?"

"So, I said that I wanted to tell you something too." She sat back down on the bed.

He pulled a stool over and sat on it, close to the bed but out of reach. "Okay, what did you want to tell me?"

"Well, Hestaphal spoke with The Gazer, you know that, right?"

"Yeah, I heard something about that."

"Okay, well, The Gazer mentioned that I end up here, in this world, whenever I dream at night."

"Okay?"

"So, that means I can see you again, dummy."

"Oh! Why didn't you just say that?"

"Because I figured you could reason it out yourself. I guess I was wrong though. I'm going to be leaving right away, so I just wanted to say goodbye for now."

"Okay. When should I expect to see you next?"

"The next time I sleep, I guess, so probably in a day or maybe a little less. I can't imagine I'll be tired after sleeping for almost three months, so I probably won't go to sleep for a while."

"Okay. So, I guess this is goodbye then."

"Yeah, I guess it is. Goodbye, Taivna."

"Goodbye, Violet."

On the way out, she gave him a peck on the cheek that she had smacked and tucked something into his hand.

After she had left, he looked at what she had put in his hand. It was a piece of paper wrapped around something. He unrolled the paper, revealing the coloring stone inside, and a note on the inside of the paper.

"Keep the drawing that's in the washroom, I told you before that it's my house. Whenever you look at it, think of me, because that's where I'll be.

I'll miss you
-Violet"

***

Hestaphal was in the courtyard when Violet got outside. He was talking to the same Elf that he had been before. When she came over, they said goodbye and Hestaphal turned to her.

"Okay, you ready to go now?"

"Yeah." Violet noticed black feathers in his hair.

"Okay, let's get going though. It's a long walk, which is why we're flying."

"What's with the feathers in your hair? You didn't have them there earlier."

"Oh, those? Sometimes remnants of the form I take on can carry over. Those are probably raven feathers." He said with a grin.

"Raven feathers... Wait. There was a raven outside of my window earlier... You! You were spying on me, weren't you?!"

"I'm sorry, but the temptation was too much. I wanted to know what you guys would talk about, so I decided to go and sneak a peek. I sure didn't expect what I saw."

Violet flushed. "You better not tell anyone!" she whispered angrily.

"Don't worry, I won't." He said while laughing. "Those were some pretty funny ways of sitting though, don't you think?"

"Can we leave already?" She asked, feeling the embarrassment starting to flourish in her cheeks.

"Sure thing." He answered while struggling to contain his laughter. He turned into a Griffin, laying down for Violet to climb onto his back, and they took off towards the mountains.

* * *

They saw the temple in the distance. They had been flying for a couple hours now and Violet had managed to avoid embarrassing topics for the whole flight.

The afternoon sun was beginning to set, painting the far horizon purple and littering it with stars. The temple didn't look like anything special on the outside, but from its titanic doorway a light was shining across the mountains in front of it.

They began their descent, gradually coming closer to the stone platform before the doorway. When they finally landed, the light had changed color. It had gone from white to purple.

Violet got off the Griffin, who soon turned back into Hestaphal, and waited for him to lead the way. Violet could feel the chill wind against her neck, but it did not make her cold. Nothing could at this point, even if she was able to feel cold in this world. Her heart was racing; soon, she would be going home.

Hestaphal led the way into the temple, Violet following close behind. The temple blocked out the sun now; it had dropped below the mountain range, but the platform was lit up from the light emanating from the temple's doorway.

When they entered the great building, Violet noticed the walls, they shined a brilliant purple. When she looked to the back of the temple, she could hardly make out any definition of the room.

Hestaphal led her to the back of the temple, unfazed by the blinding light. Violet was covering her eyes for the last half of the walk.

They arrived at the very back of the temple and were met with an ethereal voice, it sounded inexplicably similar to how cashmere felt.

"Ah, Shapeshifter, I'm glad to see your safe return. And you have brought the girl as planned. Perfect. Violet Glendale, I do believe this our first time meeting face to face. I am The Gazer; the warden for this and many others."

"Hello. Um, I can't exactly open my eyes without being blinded right now. Is there anything you could do about that by chance?"

"Oh, yes, my apologies." The light dimmed. "I sometimes forget that the mortal eye proves to be feeble when faced with such intensity of light."

Violet opened her eyes now, seeing the glowing form of a wingless Dragon. She recognized it from when she had seen it in the Observatory. "That's much better, thank you."

"So, you have come to be sent home now." A map of stars manifested in front of the Astral Dragon. "Have you enjoyed your three months in our world? Not causing too much trouble, I hope." He started to look through the map, going further and further into space.

Violet looked at Hestaphal, who was watching the map. "Yes, I enjoyed my time being here, but I'm excited to get home too."

"Undoubtedly. One can only be away from home for so long before they feel sick." In the middle of the room a three dimensional picture of Earth appeared. "Does this look familiar to you?"

"Yes." Violet said, her mouth hanging open slightly. It looked so much more beautiful like this to her.

"Could you do me a favor? Find your body for me. To you it will glow like a beacon in the night, but to me, there is nothing."

The picture of Earth spun around, showing Violet the other side. In her country, there was a light shining.

"Don't be shy; come and put your hand on the light."

Violet walked forward, placing her hand against the light, it passed through the image, and she brought her hand back, wrapping it around the light.

"This works much like that magic well at the mother tree that you have been using." At this Hestaphal raised an eyebrow. The Gazer noticed. "Oh, right. You didn't know about that, now did you? Anyways, let's send you home now, shall we?"

The Astral Dragon started chanting something in an unknown language. It started out quiet, but quickly became loud, shaking the building and filling Violet's mind. The last thing Violet heard was the sound of shattering glass before she passed into darkness.

She saw nothing.

She heard nothing.

She felt nothing.

Chapter Thirty Seven

Reunion

In the hospital room, Diana was reading the new book that Bryan had brought for her. From the corner of her eye, Diana noticed movement. It wasn't from the door, but from the bed. Diana shut the book and put it aside. She moved closer to the bed, waiting. For a moment, there was nothing. Diana sat back in her chair, still watching Violet. She picked up the book and started reading again.

Another slight movement, Diana held on to the book but was looking at her daughter once more. She waited for something, anything. Just when she was about to start reading again, she noticed the flutter of eyelids and the lifting of fingers.

Violet's eyes opened up, and Diana shut the book throwing it into the other chair. She got up and stood beside the bed.

"Violet? Can you hear me, sweetie? Please, say something. Move your fingers if you can hear me."

Violet's eyes fluttered once more, then focused on Diana. "Hi, Mom." She said, a faint smile spreading across her face and a tear running down her cheek.

Diana's eyes started to cloud with tears. She wrapped her arms around her daughter and lowered herself into a hug. Her whole body was convulsing from a mix of laughing and crying. She was mumbling and kept kissing Violet's cheek from time to time.

She stood up. "Oh, Violet! I'm so glad you're okay!" She hugged her daughter again. Don't you ever leave me again, you hear me?"

"Mom, where am I? What happened?"

Doctor Lindbel came into the room, his eyes widening when he saw Violet. "When did she wake up?"

***

Doctor Lindbel ran several tests to make sure that Violet was okay. All of the injuries from the collision had healed over, and the concussion was no longer an issue. Now that the coma was over, she was as healthy as she had been three months ago.

After he established that everything was okay, the Doctor left

Diana and Violet alone.

"So, I got hit by a car?" Violet asked.

"Yes, a drunk driver when you were on a crosswalk. You did nothing wrong. Luckily, there was a witness who called an ambulance. You were brought here, we got a call at home, and we came to see what had happened." Diana started to tear up again. "You've been asleep for three months. I was so worried, I haven't left your side for more than ten minutes, ever. I'm just so glad that you're okay!" She gave her another hug. "Don't you ever do that to me again, okay? Never again."

"Okay, Mom." She answered, hugging her mother. Her own eyes were getting a bit foggy with tears again, having abated from the initial.

***

Bryan was at work when he got a phone call. He checked the phone. It was the hospital. Was this the call? Had Violet passed away in her sleep? He didn't want to pick up the phone, but unless he wanted to be worried for the rest of the day, he had to answer.

With a shaking hand, he picked up the phone, bringing it to his ear. "Hello?" He answered, his voice trembling.

"Bryan Glendale?" The receptionist asked.

"This is him." He could hardly contain his emotions.

"Could you come down to the hospital right away? Your daughter is awake."

Those four words took the weight of the world from his shoulders. "Yes, thank you. I'll be there as soon as I can." He put the phone back on the receiver. "She's okay!" was all that was going through his head. His dam of emotions broke, letting everything into his mind. He was so happy, so relieved!

He left the library in the hands of his assistant and ran outside to his car. He couldn't be at the hospital quick enough, a phrase he would have never thought he'd say until three months ago.

***

Bryan stopped by the house on the way there to pick up Peter. He told his son the news as soon as he got home, and together they could fuel an entire carnival with their happiness.

Peter didn't hesitate to shut his computer and get in the car with his dad. They left for the hospital immediately.

***

In the hospital, Violet was telling her mother about all the dreams she had had in her long sleep. She recounted the lone hill with the talking tree and how she had heard a voice from the sky. She told her about the lake with the Manticore and described the beast to her mother. She told her about Heidskun, about the first time she set eyes on the great tree, about the festival in its courtyard and about how she had met all these different races of beings that she had met. She told her about how she had to stay at the tree from the time she arrived until the day she woke up, and how boring it was most days. She withheld information about the boy she had met, because she didn't want her mother to think she was crazy; having a crush on a figment of her imagination was a little ridiculous, even to Violet.

All the while that Diana listened, she could only think of one thing; her daughter was back.

Violet continued to tell her story for a half hour, then Bryan and Peter finally arrived.

Bryan ran over to Violet as soon as he came into the room, giving her a hug that lasted almost a whole minute while exclaiming his disbelief and relief. He started to cry tears of joy.

"It's okay, dad. I'm here now." Violet comforted.

Peter stood behind his dad, waiting. He had never been very physical with his sister, not in the sense of hugs anyways, so he wasn't sure what to do when his turn came to welcome her back.

Bryan finally let go of his daughter, wiping his eyes and leaving tear stains on the shoulder of her hospital robe.

Peter stepped forward. He couldn't help but smile when he saw his sister again with her bedraggled hair. He felt a lump in his throat and couldn't say anything; he knew that if he spoke he would start crying.

Violet smiled back at him. "Are you gonna say something?" She poked at him.

He couldn't keep it together anymore. He gave her a hug and his stomach began to heave with silent sobs.

"You've always been a softy." She teased him. "I'm happy to see you too." She whispered.

Peter couldn't put his thoughts into words. He was so happy that his sister was back, his family could start living normally again; his sister would be home with him again, his mother would come home at all, and his dad wouldn't be as depressing now that they were both home. Things would go back to normal, and that meant more than anything to Peter.

A nightmare had ended for all of them, and they couldn't describe their relief for having their family together again.

Chapter Thirty Eight
Reality

Hestaphal stood in The Gazer's chamber. It was nearly pitch black now that the Dragon was fueled by only one star.

"It is done, she is home." The Gazer said, his voice sounding tired and feeble.

"How do you know?"

"I told you before, she is bound to our world. I can see her now. It's a sad reality, but she won't remember much of all of this. I told her secrets that she was not allowed to know, and the price for that is her memories."

"How much will she remember?"

"She will remember some of our people, and she will remember Heidskun. She will not remember me, and she never will." The Gazer shot Hestaphal a glare. "If any of you tell her what happened here, then there will be severe consequences." The Gazer coiled his body. "If she knew the truth about forced rest, then one of two things would happen: she would tell others and they would think she was insane, or she would tell others and they would believe her. Either outcome would change their history too much, so it is better that she does not remember it at all."

"I see." Was all he said.

"Go now, Shapeshifter. I must rest. Tell the others what I have told you today. Farewell." Sleep took him.

Chapter Thirty Nine
Home

Violet was glad to be going home to her own bed. She had had to stay in the hospital for a few days, but now that she was getting to go home, she felt much better.

Bryan and Peter had gone home to make preparations, and Diana had stayed with Violet for the few days at the hospital. After all, what were three more days after three months?

Each day Violet was tested again to make sure everything was still in working order. She passed every exam, clearing any concerns from the doctor. On the third day, after the tests, they were cleared to go home. Violet put on her clothes, the same pink skirt and white spotted shirt that she had worn last time she was awake. There were a few spots of rough mending on them where her mother had sewn the tears shut once more.

"Did you do this?" Violet asked her mother, pointing to the mended spots on her skirt.

"Yeah, I had a lot of free time in this hospital room, so I tested my hand at sewing again. It's been a long time since I actually sewed often, but I'd say I did a pretty good job for having not touched a sewing needle in so long."

Violet continued to stare at the sewn threads.

"What is it?" Diana asked.

"It's just... I told you about the Nymph Queen from my dreams right? Well, her name was Diana, I think I told you that too. She sewed the tears on my skirt in my dream too."

"I see, that's an odd coincidence."

Violet thought nothing more of it. She took her clothes to the washroom, nearly tripping on the way there. She still wasn't quite used to her own body again, but she was getting there. The hospital shower was much smaller than her own at home, but it did its job. Violet stepped into the steam filled room, the mirror was fogged up. Violet dried herself off with the towel and wiped the mirror off. She had the strangest feeling, as if she had done this same thing just yesterday. Violet dressed herself and left her hair; she didn't feel like bothering with the knots today.

Violet walked out of the washroom, followed by a wave of warm air.

"So, are you ready to go home?" Diana asked her.

"Yeah." Violet answered, her voice showing much less excitement than she actually was.

They left the hospital room, walking down the corridor towards the main entrance. They met Bryan and Peter in the main lobby, and, as a family, they got into the car. Violet got to sit in front and her dad sat in the back with Peter. The drive back was lively, they were all talking and sharing stories from the last three months. Although only one of them was truly apart from the family, they had all grown detached over the last three months.

They arrived at home without any scares. They all got out of the car and followed Violet to the door. Violet opened the door and was met with confetti and balloons.

"Surprise!"

Their entry way was filled with familiar faces. A sign had been hung from the ceiling that read "Welcome Home, Violet!" The house smelled so familiar to Violet, and she recognized most of the faces too. Her close friends were there and their parents, some of her parents' friends were there too. One face stood out above the others to her. It was Lily. They met eyes, and Violet walked into the house.

Everyone was saying hello to Violet and giving their condolences. Violet walked over to Lily and gave her a hug.

"I can't believe I was the last person to see you that day. If we had just gotten a cab or one of our parents to drive us both then none of this would have happened. I'm sorry, V." Lily was trying to hide her dampened eyes from onlookers.

"Don't worry about it Lily. It's over now. I just wish we could have had our summer together. But we've still got two weeks left of it, maybe we could put them to use after." Violet told her.

Lily was choked up, she could only answer with "Yeah" before she started crying into Violet's shoulder.

The whole afternoon, and into the evening, friends came to talk to Violet for a while, telling her that they worried about her the whole time and that they were glad that everything turned out okay.

Before the night was over, Violet wanted to go and hide away in her room, so she did. She went to her room when everyone was busy and she had an opportunity to go without being noticed. In her room, Violet laid on the bed. She was touched that everyone was being so thoughtful, but for her first day back she had just wanted to be alone with her family.

A knock came at her door.

"Who is it?" Violet called.

"It's Lily." She answered.

"It's unlocked."

The door opened and Lily came into the room. "So you just decided to run off? I guess I can't really blame you." She came in and shut the door, sitting beside Violet on the bed.

"Lily, I feel like I'm forgetting something."

"Something like what?"

Violet looked at Lily. "Do you think if I knew what it was that I forgot, I would feel like I forgot something?"

Lily frowned.

"Sorry. I know you're just trying to help, but it's just so frustrating. It feels like it's something important, but I can't think of anything that it could have been."

"Well, I guess you'll just have to stop thinking about it then." There was a brief pause. "Hey, why don't you come downstairs? Everyone wants to say goodbye to you before they leave."

"I guess I should probably go and say thanks to everyone again, shouldn't I?" Violet laid back on the bed.

"It would be the kind thing to do, yeah." A short silence passed between them. "I'll be waiting downstairs; hopefully you'll come see us off." Lily got up from the bed and walked to the door, closing it behind her as she left.

Violet sat up again, reluctant to go back to the crowd. She got up from the bed and checked the mirror; she looked the same as when she left the hospital, knotted hair and all. She opened the door to head downstairs. Going down the stairs, she hears a few voices from the main floor. She gets there in time to catch everyone at the door.

"Oh, there's the girl!" A larger man called. It was one of her dad's friends from the library.

The crowd turned to see Violet. They all waved and said goodbye in their own way on the way out. The last people to go were Lily and her parents.

"Oh! I almost forgot!" Lily ran out to her family's car, coming back with a few bags. "I managed to find your things again. No one saw them that night, so I had to get new ones, but it's no big deal. Well, go ahead; open one!" Lily said. She was bouncing with excitement.

Violet opened one of the bags and was met with a sleeveless magenta dress. She had forgot about what she had bought that day, but, seeing it now, she remembered the dress vividly. She shut the bag, and gave her friend a hug. "Thanks, Lily."

When the Hensworth family finally left, Violet and her family gathered in the living room to watch the movie they had missed out on three months ago. Her parents were adamant on picking up where they left off.

They were together again, a family.

Chapter Forty

Life

Violet's first night at home did not pass as smoothly as she had hoped. She found herself afraid to sleep without someone beside her. What if she didn't wake up again? Hours of sleep passed her by, until finally the sun was starting to rise, and she fell asleep and passed into the Dreamscape.

She woke up in the courtyard behind the mother tree. Across the field she saw Diana watering flowers, accompanied by a blond boy. Violet tried to sneak up on them, taking the long way around to avoid being in their path. She got within arm's reach and watched them for a bit. Diana wasn't using anything to water with, she made a pattern in the air with her hands and then a small cloud formed above the plant. She snapped her fingers when she was finished and the cloud dissipated. Violet tapped Diana on the shoulder first. She turned around, eyes widening when she saw Violet.

"Oh, hello, Dear!" She gave her a hug.

Taivna turned now to see Violet's head on the Queen's shoulder. He waved, and Violet waved as well behind Diana's back.

Diana let go of Violet. "So? How is it to be back in your own world?"

"I'm glad to be back home. How are things here?"

"Well, I haven't seen Hestaphal since he left with you, but that's normal. He probably went back to the Guild." She backed up and put a hand on the boy's shoulder. "Taivna here hasn't stopped talking about you. Isn't that right?" She glanced at the boy, making him nervous.

Violet giggled. She wavered, a voice being heard in her mind. "It's time to get up." It said. It was her brother trying to wake her up.

"I have to go," Violet said, "I'll be back tonight though. Someone is trying to wake me up." She winked at Taivna, who put a hand to the back of his head.

She faded out of the Dreamscape, her consciousness returning back home.

***

Peter was shaking Violet's arm and saying "Wake up."

When Violet came to, she whipped her arm out and smacked him across the face.

"Ow! What was that for?"

"Oh! Sorry, I didn't mean to. It was just reflexes."

"What, you're used to hitting people when you wake up? I'd hate to be married to you."

She smacked him again.

"Ow! Now what was that one for?"

"I wonder what." She said sarcastically.

"Whatever, I thought it was funny. Dad was calling us downstairs, so I came to wake you up. Put something on and come to the kitchen with me."

"I'm not changing with you in the room."

Peter squinted, "I never said to."

"Then wait outside." She said, pointing at the door.

When she came out of her room, Peter was waiting beside the door. They went downstairs together.

Her parents had made an omelet for them all to share. The first day passed with family board games and watching movies together.

Violet and Lily found time to go to the cabin by the lake for a few days before the summer was over. They enjoyed each other's company again. Both their families came with them, and the two families played beach volleyball and soccer against each other a few times during their stay. However, most of their stay was spent in the water with the mothers reading on the beach.

Mrs. Hensworth closed her book. "I can't imagine how you must feel to have her back." She said to Diana.

Diana closed her book as well. "Bryan and I have never been happier to have her come home. It really put life into perspective for us; something could happen to any of us at any point, so now we are determined to use the time we have with the kids as best we can. We've only got one year left with Violet until she goes to college, so we are going to make the most of it."

"It's definitely scary to think of that, about how little control we really have over things." The two mothers looked out into the lake, watching their families playing in the water. "They grow up so quickly, don't they? It seems like not even a year ago I was just holding Lillian in my arms for the first time."

"Time is a cruel master, often dragging on painful times and taking away happy ones in the blink of an eye. But, sometimes it's also the only thing that can help to heal a wound."

They both opened their books once more.

Before the summer was over, Violet's parents had one last surprise for her and Peter. One morning when they were all together in the kitchen, Bryan made an announcement.

"Violet, Peter. Both of you go have a shower and get changed."

Peter was to first to question it. "Are we going somewhere?"

Violet was curious as well.

"As a matter of fact, we are. So both of you go get ready." Bryan answered.

"Where are we going?" Both kids asked, neither of them moving yet.

"You really want to know?" He asked.

"Yeah." They both answered.

"You're both going to the dentist, now go get ready before I have to wash you with the water hose on the lawn."

"What?! I don't want to go to the dentist!" Peter said.

"Too bad, go get changed."

Neither of the kids were happy, but they obeyed and went upstairs.

They both came back downstairs a half hour later, their hair still wet.

"You both brushed your teeth, I hope?"

"Yeah." They both answered, dragging the word out.

"Okay, then go get in the car." Bryan told them.

The drive was a painful one. Neither of the kids were excited, but Violet noticed a smile creeping across her mother's face. "There's no way we're actually going to the dentist, Mom wouldn't be that happy." She whispered to her brother.

"She's hasn't stopped smiling since you got back, I don't think now would be any different." He whispered back.

"Then why is she trying to hide it?"

Peter leaned over to check. She was, her lips were being pressed together in an effort to hide it. "That is a bit weird." He answered.

The rest of the drive was quiet, apart from the low humming of the radio. Neither of the kids cared to remember where exactly the dental clinic was, but they both knew it wasn't this far away from their home.

"Where are we actually going?" Violet asked.

"The dentist, I told you." Bryan answered.

"It isn't this far away from home, I know that much."

The car turned a corner, and a little ways ahead was a sign that read "Zoo".

Violet's eyes widened. "The zoo? I thought the tickets were for back in May?"

Diana answered this time. "Your father and I found someone who bought the tickets, so yesterday we bought tickets for today. I hope you two are still excited to go."

Peter was vibrating in his seat.

Bryan dropped them off at the main doors and went to find a place to park.

They waited for him at the entrance. When he arrived, they went in as a family.

***

The first day back to school was a bit odd for Violet. Most of her classmates kept asking her how she was, a few asked her what it was like, and some didn't say anything.

It was the start of a new year at school, and Violet felt more lost than usual. With every passing day, Violet had less and less questions asked of her, until finally they stopped all together. Violet was happy, she was finally back in her own world with her friends and family, and she could still visit her other friends at night. The best of both worlds.

71512292R00093

Made in the USA
Columbia, SC
01 June 2017